Lara gave a cry and
the back of her nightgown with her hands. Her
cheeks were hot. Beads of sweat were rolling
down her cheeks.

There was a sudden burst of cool air and a
clap of thunder. Lara slowed her flailing arms
and breathed. She focused her eyes on the rise
and fall of the white curtains at the window.
There was the immediate feeling of solid bed
and soft sheets beneath her legs. The outline of
the slanted ceiling above her. The breeze blew
over her.

It was only a dream.

She'd had nightmares before she went into
rehab, but they'd been different. Dreams of
walking alone. Dreams of slight humiliations,
entrapments, and sometimes guys who overpowered her.

This dream was much more terrifying and
much more real.

MAKING OUT

Don't forget Lara

KATHERINE APPLEGATE

Pan Books

Cover photography by Jutta Klee

First published 1998 by Macmillan Children's Books
a division of Macmillan Publishers Limited
25 Eccleston Place, London SW1W 9NF
and Basingstoke

Associated companies throughout the world

ISBN 0 330 35260 1

1 3 5 7 9 8 6 4 2

A CIP catalogue record for this book is available from
the British Library.

Printed and bound in Great Britain by
Mackays of Chatham plc, Kent

Zoey

There's one question I keep asking myself. There's just one little piece of the puzzle that's missing. All I want to know is: Why?

Why would Lucas betray me?

More important, why would he lie to me about it? Why would he go to all the trouble of lying and telling me that he loves me when it's so obviously not true? Why bother?

And the same goes for Nina. Why would she continue to play the part of my best friend, when clearly my friendship meant less to her than a piece of Kleenex?

This is what I keep going over and over in my mind.

But I don't come up with any answers.

I am sitting in a window seat of an American Airlines Boeing 747 flying from Boston to San Francisco at an altitude of thirty-one thousand feet. We left Boston on time under clear skies at 9:05 this morning and will glimpse the Golden Gate Bridge sometime around 11 A.M., Pacific Standard Time. I am on my way to college. That fact seems so unreal to me. How can I be going to Berkeley when everything has just fallen apart?

It's confusing to be gazing down at Kansas,

which is what I am doing right now. It looks a little bit like a faded quilt someone laid over the flat earth.

That's what I wish it were. I wish it were a blanket on which I would sit down on and share a picnic lunch with my best friend and my boyfriend and not a huge expanse of space, one of many such spaces, separating me from everyone I've ever cared for. Separating me from everything I've ever known.

But that's what it is.

It's just another part of the distance I am crossing to get to my new life. And like it or not, that new life will not, cannot, include people like Lucas and Nina.

I refuse to think about them anymore.

I have a life to live.

One

"Welcome to Gardner Hall," the girl behind the dorm registration table said. "You're on the fourth floor in room four sixty-five." She handed Zoey Passmore two keys attached to a big plastic tag. "Your roommate is Anika Cusak from San Rafael. She's already signed in."

"San Rafael. That's sounds California-ish," Zoey said with a wry smile.

The girl looked down at Zoey's form. "And you're from Maine?" she asked.

"Right," Zoey said.

"Hope you like UC Berkeley," the girl replied with a distracted smile. "There's a meeting of new residents in the first-floor lounge at seven tonight. Incoming freshmen are required to be there."

"Thanks." Zoey grasped her duffel bag and half carried, half dragged it toward the elevator. The lobby was crammed with piles of luggage and clumps of students and parents.

Zoey felt dizzy. For a brief instant she had a

vision of a teeming universe, full of possibility and choice. The complications and hurt she'd left back on Chatham Island seemed almost like a novel she'd read once and put back on the shelf.

Almost.

She still could hardly believe that her boyfriend, Lucas Cabral (her ex-boyfriend now, she supposed), had been seeing her best friend, Nina Geiger, behind her back. She could hardly believe that the two people she trusted most in the world had betrayed her.

She could hardly believe it, but she had to.

Zoey punched the elevator button hard. She'd been fighting it all day, but she was beginning to feel a little hot behind the eyes. But this was not the moment to break down and cry. She reminded herself that she'd only learned about Nina and Lucas the night before last, although it seemed like an eternity. She needed a little time.

The elevator door opened, and Zoey blinked back tears. The long, carpeted hallway was jammed in both directions with students carrying suitcases and shoving boxes through doorways. Doors slammed. Laughter rang out. A tall girl walked by in a robe with a pink towel on her head. Zoey breathed in the smell of microwaved popcorn and followed the room number signs to

465, which was toward the end of the hall near the fire escape, where a soda machine hummed in the corner.

Zoey knocked softly on the door, then opened it slowly. A girl in black biking shorts was standing on one of the beds, tacking a poster to the wall.

"Hi," Zoey said shyly. "Are you Anika?"

"None other," the girl answered, turning around. She had shiny black hair worn in a long braid, wide-set brown eyes, and a muscular body. Silver hoop earrings grazed her healthy-looking cheeks. "Are you Zoey Passmore?"

"Yeah." Zoey lugged her suitcase in through the door, taking in the room.

There wasn't much to see. The room was a rectangular cubicle with a waxed linoleum floor, and against each of the long, opposite-facing walls was a single bed. Identical, built-in desks were squeezed in between the bed heads and the big window at the end of the room. Hooked into the wall above Anika's bed, however, was a purple-and-black racing bicycle, slightly scratched but well oiled, with carefully taped handlebars. A collection of helmets, biking shoes, and pads stuck out of the top of a cardboard box at the foot of her bed.

"Oppressive, isn't it?" Anika said.

"The room?" Zoey asked.

"Yeah." Anika grinned. "Cell block four sixty-five. Home sweet home."

Zoey smiled back. There was an intelligent, hard edge to the expression in Anika's eyes that Zoey liked immediately. "I guess we won't be inviting the entire floor over for a giant game of Twister," Anika continued.

Zoey laughed, nodding toward the bike. "Nice wall hanging."

"I'm majoring in interior decoration," Anika deadpanned. "I'm going for the rugged, out-doorsy look—what do you think of gingham curtains?"

Zoey shook her head. Anika was beginning to remind her of Nina, which was strangely comforting considering the circumstances. "Gingham clashes with linoleum."

Anika hopped down from the bed and offered Zoey her hand. "You're from Maine, right? Welcome to the West. People from the East think we're all laid-back and self-absorbed. I can't speak for others, but it's completely true in my case."

Zoey shoved her duffel bag forward with one foot and accepted Anika's handshake. "I can cope with that if you can deal with my cranky Maine stick-to-it-iveness."

"You'll be going with the flow before the

week is out." Anika climbed back up on her bed to finish pushpinning in a biking poster.

Zoey walked toward the window and looked out.

"The room's dinky, but the view's good," Anika noted. "Even my Marin County real estate agent mother approved: 'The three *L*s of real estate are location, location, location!'" she mimicked.

Zoey laughed, peered out the window, then sucked in her breath. The view *was* good. From the window she could see the Sproul Hall tower sailing over the red-tile roofs of the massive university buildings climbing up the hillside beyond. A huge iron gate marked the entrance to the campus, which opened onto a wide redbrick walk crowded with bikes and students with backpacks. In the distance she could see the Berkeley Hills, covered with eucalyptus groves, oak trees, and old houses facing west over the San Francisco Bay.

"Have you been traveling all day?" Anika asked, reaching for a container of juice.

"Yeah," Zoey said, flopping onto the empty bed. "I spent last night in Boston and caught a flight to San Francisco at nine this morning. Then I caught a shuttle van to the Oakland Sheraton and a taxi to the dorm. It worked out pretty well."

Anika sipped her juice and set it down. "You're brave."

Zoey shrugged and zipped open her duffel bag. "Well, it wasn't hard; it just took a long time."

Anika nodded, pulling a poster out of a cardboard tube. "I should have done the same thing. Gone far away to college, I mean. But the long-distance biking thing is bigger out here than on the East Coast. And I got a creative-writing scholarship. So I guess I'm stuck in the Bay Area for now."

Zoey's eyes lit up. "Really? What kind of writing do you do?"

"Poetry," Anika said. "Anyway, I try."

Zoey grimaced inwardly. Anika seemed nice, but Zoey hoped she wasn't going to end up feeling totally out of shape and uncreative living with an athletic poet.

"But don't worry. I won't spend my life here in our room composing precious works of art," Anika said, as if she'd read Zoey's mind. "I've got a cute brother who takes me surfing."

"I surf, too," Zoey volunteered.

"Wow," Anika said. "I didn't realize that blond surfer girls existed on the East Coast. You're going to fit in great."

"Well," Zoey hedged. "I *barely* surf. I've tried it and managed not to kill myself, which is a start." Zoey sat down, then laid back her head. She was suddenly overcome with exhaustion.

"My brother and I are going surfing in Santa Cruz the weekend after this," Anika said. "Why don't you come along? We've got an extra board and tons of gear. The water is totally cold and it'll probably be foggy, but it's always fun."

Zoey was beginning to realize that she was on the verge of sobbing, screaming, or possibly throwing up. She knew her weariness and jet lag were partly to blame. But she also knew that the sheer effort of blocking out Lara's revelation had taken its toll. Sure, her half sister wasn't exactly a reliable source of information. But Zoey knew there was truth in what she'd said about Nina and Lucas.

They had been acting weird—too weird—over the past couple of weeks. The whole horrible fact was just beginning to hit her, Zoey finally realized. And for a moment she couldn't think of a thing to say to Anika.

"Are you okay?" Anika asked.

"I'm just—" Zoey started, only to realize that she had no idea how to finish that sentence. *I'm just heartbroken? I'm just losing the fragile grip I have on my sanity?*

"I'm just tired," Zoey said.

Anika nodded. "Look," she said, "I'm going to go out for my usual Thursday afternoon latte;

11

I think maybe you should take a rest. My bed is already made—you can sleep in it if you want so you don't have to dig for your sheets."

Zoey looked up, hoping her relief and thanks showed on her face, and nodded wordlessly. The dorm-room door shut and she turned on her side, watching the gentle northern California light filter in through the window. Down the hallway, on the other side of the door, she could hear the hollow sounds of doors slamming and the elevator doors opening and closing. There was a burst of laughter. A toilet flushing. In the room above her sounded the bass track of a song she'd never heard before.

Zoey tried not to think about Lucas and Nina. She tried not to think about Lara's victorious smile after she'd told Zoey everything. But it was as if every thought, every other possible thought, had left her mind. She couldn't remember the lyrics to her favorite song or Einstein's theory of relativity. She could think only of her boyfriend and her best friend, whom she loved best in the world. For months Zoey had been preparing to leave them behind, but she'd always counted on having them to come home to.

She closed her eyes.

Now there would be no going home. Her home had become someplace foreign to her, populated by people she once thought she knew and now realized that she didn't.

For the first time in her life Zoey was truly alone.

"Lara!" Darla Passmore called from the backyard. "Come on down! Everyone's here!"

Lara slipped off the wrinkled bed, stuck her number-six graphite pencil between her teeth, and walked over to the window. She pushed it open and stared down at the modest concrete patio, surrounded by grass, potted geraniums, and a growing collection of Passmore friends gathered around a smoking barbecue. She leaned through the window and pulled the pencil out of her mouth. "I'll be right down."

Darla shaded her eyes and looked up, nodding. She was wearing shorts, clogs, and a sweatshirt that read Don't Do It in front. Her faded blond hair stuck out in wisps from beneath a ragged baseball cap.

Lara backed away from the window and looked into Zoey's closet, where she'd stuffed a lot of her clothes the night before—when she was sure Zoey was completely gone.

Talk about a contrast, Lara thought. She stared with amusement at the few things Zoey had left behind: a sailor-striped top, a conservative pink blazer, and two worn pairs of khaki slacks. Lara's own minimal collection consisted of either leather or denim except for a few warm weather T-shirts in black, white, or lime green.

Marilyn Manson meets Pollyanna.

Lara decided to try to make a good impression tonight at her father and stepmother's barbecue. After all, they *were* letting her stay with them. And Zoey's room was a huge improvement over the grungy apartment she'd been staying in for the past few months.

Even if it did still reek of Zoey.

Lara checked herself out in front of Zoey's full-length mirror, first running her hands through her spiky, platinum hair, then tissuing off the dark purple lipstick and replacing it with red. The last few weeks of clean living had given her cheeks a subtle glow—a welcome improvement, in addition to the benefits of feeling human in the morning instead of wasted. She threw on a tank top, tucked it into her blue jeans, and went downstairs. The only question now was figuring out how she was going to make conversation with a whole lot of adults she barely knew.

"Hi," Darla said casually as Lara entered the kitchen. Darla was now tearing up lettuce into a bowl and chatting with two women in shorts who were dumping corn on the cob into a pot of boiling water.

Clumps of summer herbs hung across the window, and all along the top of the stove were variously shaped bottles of imported olive oils, suspicious-looking spices, and jars of utensils. The refrigerator door was encrusted with magnetically held recipes, sketches, lists, newspaper clippings, and photographs.

"Lara," Darla said, "you know Midge and Lori."

"Hi," Lara said, putting her hands into her pockets.

"Would you grab the potato salad out of the fridge and bring it outside?" Darla asked, shutting off the faucet and grabbing the salad servers.

"Sure," Lara said, inching aside to make room for two kids chasing through the kitchen with a Super Soaker.

"Outside with those, gentlemen," Darla said firmly. She looked back over at Lara as she headed outside. "It's in the back on the right-hand side."

"I see it," Lara called.

Someone turned the volume up on an old record of folk songs. Lara took a deep breath. Zoey's room was great, but the whole family package was going to take some getting used to. The Passmore house was almost never empty, just like their restaurant down on the waterfront.

Her dad and Darla were the kind of people who collected friends and acquaintances instead of coins or stamps. Stray relatives. Old college friends. Even people who'd missed the last ferry. The Passmores loved everybody, and everybody loved them.

She closed the fridge with her bare foot and headed back onto the terrace. Lawn chairs were scattered throughout the small yard, and a sagging badminton net was set up near the back of the garage.

"I need a platter for this hickory-smoked chicken!" Jeff Passmore called out through a cloud of barbecue smoke. "We've got potato salad, Thai peanut noodle salad, and corn coming up in a minute, everyone."

Lara set down the potato salad on the big picnic table.

How wholesome can an afternoon get? she thought just as she felt her father's arm slip around her shoulders. He wore jeans like her and a clean T-shirt, tucked in, which showed his still decent, forty-two-year-old torso. His dark ponytail was lightly streaked with gray.

Just then a woman in a Mexican tunic hurried up and hugged his free shoulder. "Darla said you were up at four A.M. to get Zoey to Logan Airport yesterday."

That's right, Lara thought. *Because Zoey*

16

doesn't have a tough fiber in her body. She couldn't possibly stick around and take the humiliation of having a cheating boyfriend. Actually, Lara was sort of disappointed that hearing the truth about Nina and Lucas hadn't given Zoey an aneurism.

Jeff nodded, and Lara subtly slipped out of his hug. "She wanted to get to Berkeley a day earlier than she'd planned, but we couldn't get her the flight she wanted, so she ended up spending the night in Boston with some friends of ours and leaving this morning."

"Poor thing."

Jeff laughed. "Poor *us*. Darla and I got back just in time to turn around and drive Benjamin to the ferry this morning."

The woman pressed her lips together. "Of course. Benjamin's at college, too."

"Yep. Off to Columbia," Jeff answered. "It's pretty funereal around here." He grabbed Lara's shoulder. "Lucky for me I've still got one left. You've met my daughter Lara, haven't you?"

The woman smiled and took Lara's hand warmly. "Yes. Hello again. It looks like your father has made a feast for us!"

"Dig in," Jeff said as she released Lara's hand and headed toward the food.

"Benjamin's going to miss you a lot, but it'll be good to spend time together," her father said,

turning away and wiping his hands on his barbecue rag. He steered her toward the crowded
line forming around the picnic table.

"I'll miss him, too," Lara said. She picked up
a paper plate and fork, not knowing what else
to say.

Lara understood that her father wanted to
get to know her better, but she wasn't always
clear on what she had to do to accomplish this.
Plus her dad wanted to get to know *everyone*
better. Was she supposed to believe she was
special?

No matter how great her father said she was,
she would always be just Lara McAvoy: high
school dropout, sometime alcoholic, and former
drug user whose biggest accomplishment in life
so far was holding down a job for a week
straight at her dad's restaurant without screw-
ing up.

Still, Lara thought, *at least Zoey—Miss Walk-
on-water-straight-A's-perky-overachiever—is
three thousand miles away at Berkeley.* It was
going to be a lot easier not having that particular comparison staring her in the face
every day.

"Hi, Lara," she heard a woman's voice
beside her.

Lara turned as a woman in a black sundress
with gray, bobbed hair and wire-rimmed

glasses moved next to her in the food line. Lara knew she was one of the Passmores' Weymouth friends, but she couldn't remember which one. Was it the woman who supplied Passmores' Restaurant with fresh vegetables? The one who gave Darla cello lessons last summer? The ultraliberal legislator?

"I'm Sandy Krukmeyer," the woman explained. "I own an art gallery over in Weymouth."

Lara nodded. She was positive she'd met the woman before. But Lara was fairly sure she'd been soaked in alcohol at the time. Or perhaps zipped out on one chemical substance or another. It had done some pretty weird things to her memory.

"It's called the S&K Gallery," the woman said.

Lara nodded again and took a paper plate. The S&K Gallery wasn't just another tacky tourist shop selling waterfront scenes and lobster key chains. It was a serious art gallery that had regular showings of top Boston artists. Last summer Lara had seen a cutting edge collection of abstract oils there.

"Do you know it?" the woman asked politely, taking a piece of chicken with tongs.

"Yes," Lara said shyly. "I really like your gallery. I saw—um—the Spike Vaughn oils there last June."

"Weren't they great?" Sandy replied. "Jeff tells me you're interested in art, too."

Lara waved away a puff of smoke from the barbecue. "Yeah. Sort of."

"What do you do?" Sandy asked, picking up a brownie off a platter. "Oils? Drawings?"

"I like oils a lot. But lately I've been working with charcoal pencils and pastels," Lara said. She felt a sharp desire for a beer, which she pushed away. "I just did a portrait of Jeff, in fact."

"Really?"

Lara felt sick. What made her say that? The woman was obviously a successful gallery owner who knew about art. *Who do I think I am?* Lara wondered. *I'm nobody.*

"I'd like to see it," Sandy said. "I'm always interested in seeing the work of new artists."

"But I'm not really an artist," Lara said abruptly. "I just work at my dad's restaurant. I fool around with art in my spare time—because—because I just like to, I guess."

Sandy nodded with a knowing look. "What exactly do you think an artist does? It sounds to me like you qualify."

Lara coughed. The barbecue smoke stung her eyes and made her feel inexplicably anxious for oxygen. "Oh. Okay."

"If it's what you love," Sandy said, "then you must spend as much time doing it as possible. Do you understand?"

"Yes." Lara nodded, practically hypnotized by this woman's seriousness.

"Come by my gallery and talk to me sometime."

LUCAS

Dear Zoey,

WHATEVER LARA told you, it couldn't have been completely true. You wouldn't have left like that.

Trying to explain what happened when you were in D.C. is almost impossible. It happened in a split second.

It's true that I kissed Nina. We were talking. We were upset. It happened, and then it was over. I don't want to be with Nina. I want to be with you. I love you like I've never loved Anyone. You've got to understAnd this becAuse if you don't, then I don't know whAt step to tAke next.

PleAse cAll me. OR wRite me if you cAn't tAlk.

Love,
LucAs

Two

"I'm Claire Geiger."

"Hi, Claire," the woman behind the sixth-floor registration desk said. According to her plastic name tag, she was an MIT Barron Hall Women's Dorm Resident Assistant named Julie Sontay. She was a tiny girl with wiry brown hair, round glasses, and a clipboard with papers, which she was now flipping through for Claire's name.

"Geiger," Claire said impatiently, pushing back a strand of her long dark hair. "The form you sent me said room six-oh-three, Barron Hall."

"Uh-huh," she said, grabbing several forms and information sheets, then stapling them together.

Claire shifted, her eyes darting back to her luggage. At least things had gone smoothly on the drive from Chatham Island to Boston. She and her father had driven down together. Mercifully they had said good-bye in the lobby, where they were able to find a huge cart for her stuff.

Now she was hovering protectively over her eight matching suitcases, standing garment bag, boxed computer, and stereo.

"Geiger," the RA repeated.

Claire rolled her eyes impatiently.

The RA finally handed her the paperwork and two large keys. "Okay. You're in six-oh-three at the end of the hall to your right. Your roommate's name is . . . ," she began, and flipped through her papers again.

Claire cocked an eyebrow. "I don't have a roommate."

The RA pushed her glasses up on her nose and looked confused. "Everyone in the dorm does. Especially this year. We're completely jammed." She continued her flipping.

Claire smiled sweetly. "I'll wait while you check for me," she replied evenly. "Just to be sure."

The RA flipped back through her paperwork, ran her finger down a list, then stopped. "You've been assigned to a single room," she said slowly. She stood up and examined a laminated diagram of the sixth floor on the wall behind her. "Well, not exactly."

Claire was overcome with momentary horror. *My God,* she thought, *did they actually come up with someone who matched my roommate application?* She'd deliberately filled out the housing compatibility form to make herself sound like a maniac. She knew, that is, she'd *hoped* that after reading it, the housing people wouldn't be able to match her with a single woman at the Massachusetts Institute of Technology. "What do you mean?" she demanded.

The RA turned around. "What I mean is that you have been designated a single room, but the room isn't really a single."

"It isn't?"

"No. It's actually a large double room. But the housing department assigned you to it without a roommate," the RA said, beginning to look harassed. "I don't know how that happened."

"Me, either," Claire said lightly, gripping the luggage cart. "I can't imagine how." She felt a surge of intense pleasure. Her gamble had paid off.

Claire pulled her luggage to the end of the dim hallway, where several girls were squeezing their suitcases, sports equipment, and computers into shoe–box–size rooms. When she reached room 603, Claire unlocked the door, opened it, and sighed with satisfaction. Her room was at least twice the size of the others, with two single beds, two wooden desks, two dressers, and bookshelves that nearly reached the ceiling.

She drew the drapes and felt her smile

broadening. Her view was to the east, over the Charles River, Boston Harbor, and Massachusetts Bay beyond, shining in the late afternoon light. Below she could see Cambridge's buildings and busy streets, choked with bicyclists, joggers, and the vibrant green of city trees. Behind her, out of view, was Harvard University.

"Well," Claire whispered. "I guess this is home."

Claire looked up at the sky. High, cirrus clouds. Winds from the northeast. Low pressure. Storm on the horizon. Rain by early morning, she predicted.

"Hi. I'm Felicia Sherritt," the girl said, holding out her hand eagerly.

"Hi, Felicia," Aisha said, setting her suitcase down inside the tiny dorm room the Harvard housing authorities had assigned her. She and her fiancé, Christopher Shupe, had just said good-bye in the lobby, and Aisha's eyes were still wet with tears.

Felicia ducked down her head, as if to look into Aisha's eyes. "Are you okay?" she asked, moving a little closer and reaching out to touch Aisha's arm.

Aisha gave her a grateful smile. "Yes. Yes, I'm okay. Thanks. Just—leaving-home stuff."

"I know what you mean," Felicia said with a sympathetic nod. "I wasn't as ready as I thought I was, either." She glanced at Aisha's heavy luggage. "Do you need help with your suitcase?" she asked.

Aisha was impressed by how helpful her new roommate seemed. "No, thanks," she said as she swung her suitcase up on the narrow bed. Aisha turned to get a good look at Felicia. Felicia was tall and slender, with silky blond hair twisted casually at the back of her head. Though she wore only faded blue jeans and a fitted black T-shirt, there was something elegant about the way she held herself.

Aisha looked around the room. Her dorm was one of the older ones on the campus, a long, three-story structure with radiators, ancient furniture, musty carpeting on the stairways, and charming paned windows that looked over a stately quad area.

"It's kind of a small room," Felicia said, "but I'm really easy to live with—I swear!"

Aisha laughed. Felicia was right—the room was practically a small closet, no more than ten by fifteen feet, barely big enough for the beds and two small desks. The dressers were in the closet, which left little room for hanging anything. "It's a lucky thing I don't have many clothes."

"You're smart," Felicia said, opening one of the closets to reveal a space crammed with sweaters, skirts, slacks, and shoes. "I brought everything I've ever owned. Including stuff I haven't worn since I was in the third grade."

Aisha laughed again. Felicia was making her feel better already. Maybe Aisha had left some good friends behind, but her new roommate was evidence that there were plenty of new friends just waiting to be met.

It was time for a new beginning.

Benjamin Passmore turned up Columbus Avenue toward campus after a few hours of strolling through CD stores and generally taking in the atmosphere of New York City. His parents had driven him to the ferry from Chatham Island, Maine, that morning and had dropped him off with merciful restraint—possibly because they were exhausted from their early morning delivery of Zoey to Logan Airport just the day before that.

Now he was intoxicated by the noisy carelessness of the city. Images and lights and colors bombarded his eyes. Dust and exhaust blew into his lungs.

He turned off Columbus Avenue past a violin shop, a Greek restaurant, and a rare-books store until he could see the university's big ironwork entrance from the street. He turned in there, feeling as if he'd entered yet another dimension. Columbia was big and monumental, with statues flaring importantly out of fountains, brick pathways rimmed with hedges, and streams of students who looked like they had something big on their minds.

Nina would love this place, Benjamin thought, almost without realizing it. Nina Geiger. He discovered, somewhere in the pit of his stomach, that he missed her. Really missed her. Probably more than anyone else on that island.

He took the stairs to his third-floor room and unlocked the door. It was pitch-black inside, and he flicked on the light.

"Hey," his roommate, Tom Cooney, complained from the depths of the curtained room. He was from Seattle and into experimental filmmaking and Carl Jung. "Turn off the fluorescents. I'm watching the final two minutes of PBS's Bergman retrospective."

Benjamin looked at his roommate, who was sprawled on his back, staring at the small TV he'd installed on the shelf next to the window. "Who?" he asked.

"Ingmar Bergman," Tom said slowly, craning his neck toward the door. "As in extraordinary Swedish filmmaker?"

"Never heard of him," Benjamin lied, rolling

his eyes and flicking off the switch. His roommate was turning out to be a major pain—a thin, pretentious guy with a goatee and closely cropped dark hair.

"Where did you say you were from?" Tom asked with a yawn.

"North Harbor, Maine," Benjamin replied, closing the door. He stood still for a moment, trying to get his bearings. The only thing he could see was a flickering square of gray on the other side of the room.

Four steps to the bed, three more steps to the window.

Benjamin found his old blind-wonder-boy instincts kicking in, and it annoyed him.

"And what do you do for entertainment there?" Tom asked as the credits began to roll up on the TV screen. "Get together with the pickup truck crowd for lobster bakes and stone-throwing contests on the beach?"

"Only when we're not having tractor races," Benjamin said evenly, deftly falling back on his bed. He slipped his hands behind his head and stared up into the darkness.

"Give me a break, Passmore," his roommate grunted. Then he turned on the light over his desk and faced Benjamin, a slight smile on his face. "So, what's happening down there on Columbus Avenue?"

Benjamin shrugged. He wanted to continue his subtle harassment, but the sudden light made his eyes ache. He closed his eyes, then opened them slowly, trying to adjust. "Checked out some CD stores. A camera shop. Generally hung out."

Tom rummaged through a cardboard box on his bed and pulled out a *New York Times*. "There's a showing of *The Incredible Shrinking Man* tonight at the Anthology Film Archives. You interested?"

"Isn't that with Arnold Schwarzenegger?" Benjamin said. "He's my favorite actor."

Tom stared at him. "Right," he said quietly.

Benjamin smiled to himself, relishing the idea that he'd found a way to rattle his roommate. He closed his eyes to think. Then opened them. There it was again. The darkness in the left eye, as if a shade had been pulled over it. A stabbing pain behind the retinas.

"When are you leaving?" Benjamin asked, digging his shoe off with the toe of the other.

"Right now," Tom said. "The place is way downtown."

The light dimmed again. The pain worsened. Maybe it was a sign he should slow it down, but then, he didn't come to New York City to close his eyes. He came here to open them.

Still, it was impossible. He couldn't stare at a

bright screen in a darkened movie house for two hours. "Sorry," he finally said. "I'm going to stick around here tonight."

"Uh-huh," Tom replied. "Well, I'll let you know the next time I'm going for a showing of *Conan the Barbarian*."

Benjamin waited, eyes closed, as Tom put his stuff together. Seven years in the dark and he could pick out his roommate's movements down to the last detail. The search for the wallet. The combing of hair. Change in the pocket. Check out the window.

"See you later," Benjamin said as his roommate left. And he hoped that it was true.

Three

Lucas Cabral had been setting lobster traps since 5 A.M. His knuckles were bleeding, and a cold, blowing fog was whipping over the water. It was Indian summer. Although it was freezing, Lucas knew that the sun would emerge in a few hours, immense and gold, from behind Allworthy Island.

He threw the last trap overboard and let its green-and-red float bob up to the top. Water slapped against the side of the boat.

It was Monday morning.

Five days since he'd last seen Zoey, her face hard and pale on the deck of the ferry as it pulled out of the North Harbor dock. The memory of how she had turned away from him made him feel physically ill.

"What are you doing right now, Zoey?" Lucas asked the wind.

He pulled up the last trap, baited it, and threw it back in the water. Then he pulled up anchor and walked back up to the helm. The ancient ignition system took five attempts before the engine kicked in, but a few minutes later he was headed west around the southern end of Chatham Island and on toward Weymouth. "Please pick up the phone," Lucas muttered, letting the cold wind blow through his hair. "Just pick up the phone tonight and call me."

Of course, there was one really good question he needed to answer before Zoey *did* call, if in fact she did. And that was: What the hell was he supposed to say?

That was the problem.

Viewed in a certain light, Lucas thought that what he had done with Nina was no big deal. He had kissed her twice. This wasn't some big torrid affair. It wasn't the type of thing that won you the Boyfriend of the Year Award, either, but on some level Lucas felt that Zoey was blowing this thing totally out of proportion.

Of course, he wasn't about to tell Zoey that.

What he had in mind was more along the lines of groveling.

He loved Zoey, but she didn't come without her own human faults, such as a certain amount of perfectionism and hypocrisy. Did her thoughts ever drift back, for instance, to the time he found her with Aaron Mendel last winter in a passionate, moaning lip lock? Aaron

Mendel, possibly the world's worst excuse for a human being. Did she ever stop to think how it made him feel to see her rolling among the twisted bedsheets with *him*, his hands groping up her half-unbuttoned shirt?

Of course, Lucas didn't plan to mention that, either. He didn't want to fan the flames of her anger any higher than they already were.

Although Lucas didn't love Nina the way he loved Zoey, he knew Nina had a deeper capacity for forgiveness than Zoey did. Nina accepted the dark and damaged side of her character, and she could do the same for others.

Lucas pulled his knit cap down over his ears and watched the low white cliffs of the mainland draw near. A package of his dad's tobacco still lay on the narrow shelf over the helm, half full and rolled up, along with a small penknife, a broken pencil, and a pad he used to keep track of his catch.

Lucas gripped the wheel, and his dad's harsh voice came back to him. *Steer it right into the wind, Lucas. It's not going to bite you.* He shuddered. This man was supposed to be his family? Zoey and Nina knew Lucas better than his dad ever had. And now his dad was dead, Zoey was gone, and Nina was acting moderately bizarre.

A half hour later Lucas had moored at the

Weymouth dock and had sold his catch to his dad's old buyer, Harry Nicholas. Actually Lucas had a pretty good haul for the season. A decent two dozen lobsters, and he'd snagged a cod for his mom. But after gas and expenses the fifty or sixty bucks he took in from his buyer wasn't much. Maybe enough for food for him and his mom, but not enough for the long term. The house was paid for with his dad's life insurance. But what about the days when the fishing wasn't so great? What if his mom got sick? What then?

A few months ago Lucas was making plans for the upcoming year at the University of Maine. Now he was making plans for how to pay for his dinner.

He shook his head, stuck the cash in his wallet, and washed off at the Weymouth dock faucet.

"How's your mother getting on, Lucas?" came a voice behind him.

Lucas turned around. The gray-haired man standing on the dock next to him was an old fishing friend of his father. In his rubber fishing trousers and frayed plaid shirt, he looked eerily like his dad, which sent a chill through Lucas.

"She's doing okay, Samuel; thanks for asking." Lucas turned back to the faucet.

"Don't know if you're interested, but there's a fellow working out at the old Blue Rock Lighthouse," Samuel told him. "Needs some help."

Lucas pulled a rag out of his back pocket and wiped his hands. "The lighthouse? It's been closed since I was a kid."

"Some kind of restoration project," Samuel said, putting his hand heavily on Lucas's shoulder. "It's a government project, so you know the pay'd be steady."

Lucas let out a laugh. "Steadier than the lobsters are right now, huh?"

Samuel let out a half smile, grunted, and stuck a pipe into his mouth. "Might want to check it out, son."

Lucas turned and headed down the long wooden pier past the jumble of gillnetters and lobster trawlers. The town of Weymouth sloped slightly up from the port-side section of town, which was lined with closed-up galleries, shops, and seafood restaurants. There was the faint but unmistakable smell of coffee and bacon from the waterfront cafés. A few banners celebrating upcoming Labor Day fluttered from the ferry dock moorings.

Another block and Lucas was in the garage where the family's pickup was kept. His pickup now, he supposed, since his mother rarely left the island. Still, it was barely running, and he wasn't even sure if the insurance was paid on it.

Lucas rumbled down Independence Avenue and turned left onto the two-lane highway that headed north up the coast. After a few miles he could see the lighthouse in the clearing fog.

When he was a kid, he always used to love watching the roll and blink of its light at night from his bedroom window. Zoey loved it, too, Lucas thought miserably. He remembered how once they had driven up there together, climbed along the rocky bank surrounding the lighthouse, and stared out at the sea.

Lucas shook away the thought as he turned down the rocky lighthouse road and parked. He forced himself not to think of the way Zoey looked climbing down those rocks—slender, windblown, and happy in her purple anorak and hiking boots. He used to love the way her skin flushed in the cold air. The steady blue of her eyes. He loved her so much, to have her think he cared for anyone more than her was unbearable to him.

Stop torturing yourself, he thought. *What good does it do now?*

Lucas got out of the truck and slammed the door. The Blue Rock Lighthouse was a stubby, cone-shaped structure only about forty feet high and made of whitewashed stone. The lantern's roof and walkway were dark metal, and two windows were punched into the side of the tower facing him.

A sturdy-looking keeper's dwelling stood nearby, and there were several outbuildings, surrounded by weathered tufts of grass and a chipped No Trespassing sign swinging on a chain.

"Anyone home?" Lucas shouted into the battered wooden door at the base of the lighthouse. Inside, the walls once plastered white were now cracked and yellowed. A rusted spiral staircase wound up the inside of the wall.

"Up here!" a deep voice called out from above. "The staircase is strictly an at-your-own-risk proposition, but feel free to come up if you're feeling lucky."

Lucas squinted into the sun shining down through the top window in the lighthouse, about three stories up. He could barely make out a guy in a plaid shirt poised on a rack of scaffolding. There was a sign on a metal chain drawn across the first step that read Hazardous—Do Not Enter. Lifting it with his finger, Lucas ducked under it and headed upward.

"Watch out for that third landing," the voice boomed. "Someone tried to bolt it back in with a staple gun about twenty years ago."

Lucas laughed. "Sounds like the state of my boat."

"A boatman in our midst?" the guy asked as Lucas neared him by the winding stairs. Now that he was closer, he could see that the man was broad shouldered and tanned with short, dark hair. The slight gray at his temples was the only clue to his age, which Lucas guessed to be in the midforties range. Like Zoey's dad.

"For now, I guess," Lucas said. "I'm working my dad's trawler for a while." He hesitated. "To make money for college."

The guy stuck his electric drill in his tool belt and started down the scaffolding. "Your dad's idea—or yours?"

"You could say it was my dad's idea," Lucas said.

The man looked sharply over his shoulder, then hopped off the bottom rung of the scaffolding onto the metal grate walkway where Lucas was now standing. He shook Lucas's hand. "I'm Guy Hoffman."

"Lucas Cabral."

Guy crossed his arms over his broad chest and smiled. "What brings you up here, Lucas?"

"Well." Lucas cleared his throat. "I saw Samuel Maccone down at the docks earlier. He told me you were looking for some help."

Guy grinned and nodded. "Oh, yeah. Samuel. Crusty old guy."

"Yeah. He's a regular baguette."

Guy laughed, then turned serious. "You got construction experience, Lucas?"

"Not exactly," Lucas replied. "My dad used to take me around on his odd construction jobs in the off-season," he went on. His gaze traveled up the smooth inner walls to the walkway surrounding the huge lantern several yards above him. When Lucas was a kid, he was fascinated by how the lens could magnify the intensity of the lighthouse's small light so that boats miles away could see it through fog.

Guy rubbed the side of his face.

"But I know how to get up early every weekday morning and work hard all day," Lucas told him. "I know the weather, and I know the people around here. I'm pretty handy with simple jobs. And I've been staring at this lighthouse since I was a kid."

Guy touched the wall. "It's a beauty, isn't it? Built in the 1850s. It's not used anymore, but that's a fourth-order Fresnel lens up there. When I'm done here, this lighthouse will be automated and totally operational."

Lucas nodded. The last of the morning fog had just blown off. Now the view stretched a hundred miles over the slate blue Atlantic.

"You got tools?"

"Yeah."

Guy stared at Lucas evenly.

Lucas leaned up against the window. "It's great up here. I haven't been up since a field trip I took with my fourth-grade class." He pointed southeast to Chatham Island, a smooth, three-mile-long stretch of green in the choppy sea. "That's where I live. In North Harbor, on the other side of that island."

"I'm going to need help here for the next six months or so," Guy said. "The spiral staircase has to be brought up to safety standards, and the interior walls need repair. After the lighthouse is done, the federal grant calls for renovation of the keeper's dwelling. That'll be the fun part."

Lucas stroked the rusted metal railing and shook it a little to test its strength. "Could use some reinforcement, all right," he said absently.

Lucas's mind was filled with so many thoughts that he was actually surprised by the sound of Guy's voice. "Common sense, brute strength, and reliability are more important to me than experience right now," Guy said. "I'll try you out for two weekends—eight hours on Saturday and Sunday at fifteen bucks an hour, if you're interested."

Lucas turned and stared. Guy was smiling.

He seemed decent enough, and Lucas definitely needed the money. Plus there were worse things than spending time up in an old lighthouse—way up above everything else, looking out to sea.

Maybe he'd even learn something useful.

The 4 P.M. Weymouth–North Harbor ferry cut its engines, and Nina Geiger felt the usual sagging momentum as the boat began its slow, sloshing maneuver into the public dock.

Turning her head slightly, she instinctively glanced up to the right, where the town of North Harbor sloped up into a pine-fringed ridge on the west side of Chatham Island.

During her Nina–Benjamin Passmore days (which, she had to remind herself, had ended not so long ago, thanks to Benjamin), it had been her habit to lock her gaze onto the Passmore house as the ferry began its slow turn around North Harbor's breakwater. There was its weathered gray siding, the three dormers, the five trees, and the weathered wind sock that blew from the arbor on the back patio.

Benjamin's home. Zoey's home.

She forced herself to look away.

Nina slipped one of her trademark Lucky Strikes out of her purse, stuck it between her lips, and kept it there, unlit, as she walked down the metal stairs from the top deck and onto the gangway on the starboard side of the bow. As she had ten thousand times before she walked up the wooden dock to Exchange and started to make her usual left turn toward Lighthouse Road.

Then she saw him.

Lucas was sitting behind the wheel of his family's weathered pickup, the elbow of his jean jacket sticking out the driver's-side window, as if he'd been waiting for a while.

Nina crossed the street slowly, hiking her book pack up on her shoulder. It wasn't until she'd reached the far side of the street that she realized how nervous she was. *Maybe he won't see me,* she thought irrationally. *Maybe he won't even notice I'm here. I'll just keep my head down and—*

"Hi," Lucas said quietly. He was listening to a weather report on the pickup's radio. Nina took in his tousled blond hair and the dark eyes that were looking at her very steadily. She was tempted to keep on walking, to just go home. But she couldn't think of any way to do that without hurting Lucas's feelings, so she stopped.

"Hi," Nina said.

"How'd the first day go?"

Nina rested her arm on the truck's side-view mirror. *We're going to engage in small talk?* she wondered. But then, it was probably better than anything else they could discuss, she figured. She decided to play along. "The usual stuff. Mrs. Keenan sucks. I'm stuck working for The Buzzard in the school office for second and third period every day. And everyone's freaked about these fitness tests we've got in gym tomorrow. Calculus was okay."

"Josephson," Lucas said absently. "I had him for calculus last year."

Nina looked at him. "All the teachers are the same, but without you guys it's just so . . . different."

Lucas looked away and rubbed his chin. "Yeah, well, I guess nothing ever stays the same."

Nina felt a clutch at her throat. What was she supposed to say to that?

"Hey," Lucas said, nodding toward the passenger door. "Want a ride? I brought the pickup over on the ferry to haul some stuff for my mom."

Nina shrugged. "For four blocks? I don't know; I could use the exercise for the fitness test tomorrow."

Lucas turned and looked at her suddenly, and his eyes were full of something—Nina didn't know what—that made her walk around the front of the truck and climb in next to him.

Lucas started the engine and shifted into reverse. Nina stared at the sinewy muscles in his forearm but looked away as he headed down Dock Street, then south onto Leeward Drive.

"This isn't the way to my house," Nina said, then rolled her eyes at the obviousness of that remark.

Lucas shrugged, glancing her way briefly. "You want to go home?"

"No."

Nina stuffed her backpack under her feet and took the Lucky Strike out of her mouth. She leaned back her head and sighed. Leeward Drive ran along the island's west coast, with a view of the mainland and the waves lapping up on the rocky beaches below.

"I got a job today," Lucas said, breaking the silence.

Nina twisted around in the seat to face him, relieved that he'd managed to find something to talk about that wasn't Zoey. "I thought you already had a job. On the boat. Do you mean you have *another* one?"

Lucas smiled, as if he were really pleased by her excitement. "Yeah. But I can do this job on the weekends—if it works out."

Nina nudged his shoulder. "What is it? Tending bar or something?"

"Restoring the Blue Rock Lighthouse," Lucas

said. "The guy who's working on it just hired me on the spot."

"Just like that?" Nina exclaimed. "He just looked at you and said—hey, I want you?"

Lucas turned and looked at her, and she prayed that he wouldn't notice the flush creeping rapidly all over her face. *Way to go, smooth talker,* she chided herself. *That sounded really great, considering the situation.* She briefly thought about rephrasing her last question but decided that any attempt to smooth it over would only make her blunder more obvious, so she remained silent. Lucas turned his attention back to the road.

"Yeah. Well, I mean, I told him a few things, but not much. I think we kind of clicked."

"Great!" Nina said instantly, and with too much enthusiasm. *Oh, Lord, I've developed inappropriate response syndrome,* she thought. "I mean, that's really wonderful; I'm proud of you." Nina cringed. *I'm proud of you?* Was she his mother now? Nina was so embarrassed that she actually let out a small gurgle, which only made her feel like a bigger idiot. She banged her forehead against the window.

Lucas looked at her, then stretched his forearm out straight on the steering wheel, tucked in his chin, and stared stubbornly back at the road. "We've got to talk, Nina."

Nina turned to face the road, too. She didn't really want to *talk* because she knew *talking* meant talking about Zoey, and she just wasn't ready to talk about Zoey yet.

Nina leaned her head back on the top of the pickup seat. She said nothing. What was there to say?

Lucas abruptly pulled over onto a narrow vista point at the side of the road. Then he turned off the engine and stuffed his hands into his pockets. "Nina," he said, and then stopped. Lucas paused for a moment, looking out at the water. Then he said it again, only softer this time. "Nina."

Tears sprang to her eyes. "I miss her so much, Lucas," Nina whispered.

"Yeah. So do I."

Because her head was tilted back, the tears ran down her temples and trickled into her hair. "I'm scared to death to call her," Nina blurted. "She's going to be so angry. . . ."

"I guess we need to give her some time," Lucas said dully.

Nina nodded silently, then brushed a stray tear away with her cuff.

"Have you written her?" Lucas wanted to know.

"Not yet," Nina whispered. "Somehow that seems even harder than calling."

Lucas turned around in the seat and looked at Nina seriously. "Write to her. It's a good way of telling her what you need to say while giving her some space. It may be hard for Zoey to forgive, but I think she will, eventually. At least I hope so."

"Have *you* written her?" Nina asked abruptly before she could stop herself.

Lucas drew back, and Nina could see the hurt in his eyes. "Yes, I did. I—I just told her what happened. I told her my side of the story, I guess."

Nina bit her lip, agonized. "How could she listen to Lara?" Nina pleaded. "She doesn't even *like* Lara. She wouldn't trust anything *else* Lara said. Why didn't she come to us if she wanted to know the truth?"

Lucas gripped the steering wheel, and Nina could see the muscles clenching in his jaw. "Write to her, Nina. Let's just both keep writing to her. Tell the absolute truth, and don't let her think we've forgotten her. It's the only way."

"Yeah," Nina said with a deep, tearful sigh. "I guess you're right."

Four

Above, Lara could see the snow-tipped peaks, ringed with boulders and green meadows. Higher and higher she climbed above the smoky valley, though she didn't know why she was hurrying or where she was headed.

The steep path climbed onto a slope filled with nodding wildflowers. And although the air was thinner now, Lara felt a strange energy propelling her forward.

Distant figures appeared on the rocks ahead. She pushed harder, feeling heat on her back and the cool of the snows on her face. Gradually she realized that the figures were Mr. and Ms. Passmore, and they were waving to her, as if they were crying for help.

Lara waved and began running forward on the path toward them. Though the heat on her back was intense, the temperature ahead was cool, and tears began to freeze in the corners of her eyes. Still, when she looked back down the path, she saw that the smoke from the valley was surging up the hillside. Flames began to jump from the trees below onto the grasses bordering her path. Smoke began to fill her lungs. Fire licked her heels.

As she approached the Passmores she screamed for them to join her on her escape to the mountaintop, where the fires couldn't reach them. But as she looked into their faces she saw that they were helpless, their feet strangely stuck to the ground like statues.

As she took her next breath she felt the smoke fill her lungs and the sting of blowing sparks on the back of her shirt. She began to pass them, realizing that she wasn't strong enough to carry them. Their cries cut through her heart but were soon silenced by the roar of the flames and rushing smoke that converged on them.

Lara gave a cry and sat up in Zoey's old bed, desperately brushing the back of her nightgown with her hands. Her cheeks were hot. Beads of sweat were rolling down her cheeks.

There was a sudden burst of cool air and a clap of thunder. Lara slowed her flailing arms and breathed. She focused her eyes on the rise and fall of the white curtains at the window to her right. There was the immediate feeling of solid bed and soft sheets beneath her legs. The outline of the slanted ceiling above her. The breeze blew over her.

It was only a dream.

Lara slipped out of bed and shut the window, then slid back on the bed, still trying to catch her breath. She'd had nightmares before she went into rehab, but they'd been different. Dreams of walking alone. Dreams of slight humiliations, entrapments, and sometimes guys who overpowered her.

This dream was much more terrifying and much more real.

Lara turned on her side and looked at Zoey's digital clock radio, which glared 6 A.M. in bright green. Her father's shower was running, and she knew he was due down at the restaurant by six-fifteen. He hadn't asked for her help, but she knew he could use it, with the upcoming Labor Day crowds. Breakfasts at Passmores' were popular with the island crowd all through the off months, even on rainy Tuesday mornings like this one.

She kicked off the sheets and pulled on a pair of jeans and a T-shirt she'd left hanging on the back of Zoey's desk chair. Since she'd showered the night before, all she had to do was brush her teeth and slip into a pair of comfortable clogs. A few minutes later she was dressed and in the kitchen, pouring coffee.

"What are you doing up?" her dad asked, strolling in.

"I woke up early," Lara said.

He frowned as he poured his own coffee into an earthen mug. "Was that you I heard?"

"What?" she asked, trying to sound nonchalant.

Mr. Passmore gave her a sidelong glance. "I thought I heard a cry—I don't know. Something."

Lara shrugged. "I had a dream." Her eyes lifted slightly from her cup, testing his reaction. "Kind of a bad dream, actually."

"Mmmm," he said, pulling cereal out of a cupboard. "Maybe it was the leftover clam dip Mildred Hanke brought to the barbecue last week."

Lara laughed softly. She could tell from his joke that he didn't want to pry, and she appreciated it.

"Sorry. Mildred's great. It's just that the little pimentos on top . . ." Her dad shook his head and laughed, too. "They cracked me up."

"Do you want help this morning at the restaurant?" Lara asked.

Her dad grinned. "Are you kidding? I can never get anyone to do this shift with me." He set down the cereal box with a thud and pushed it away. "Let's eat down at the restaurant. The food's better there."

"Okay."

"Do you feel like walking?" her dad asked. "The van's a disaster area."

Lara nodded and followed him out of the kitchen. She slipped on one of Ms. Passmore's old sweatshirts from the hall closet and stepped out into the chilly morning. The thunderstorm had slowed to a trickle and looked like it would clear out fairly soon.

Mr. Passmore picked up a stick and threw it over their fence before opening the front gate. "Your mom used to have bad dreams, too."

Lara felt an unfamiliar pang of embarrassment. She and her dad had barely ever talked about her mother. When Lara was growing up, her mother's only name for him had been *thesonuvabitch*, which was why Lara hadn't exactly been clamoring to meet him six months ago, when Benjamin tracked her down in Boston.

Now she was beginning to understand how wrong her mother had been. Not wrong as if she'd made an ordinary, forgivable mistake. But big-time wrong. The kind of wrong that had messed with Lara's head in a possibly permanent way. She'd lost her chance to grow up halfway normally, like Zoey and Benjamin had, instead of being dragged from boyfriend to Boston apartment to boyfriend like a needless piece of luggage.

A dog barked behind a weathered picket fence. In the distance the early morning ferry was pulling around the breakwater. Her father seemed to accept her silence.

"Remind me to check the post office box later," Mr. Passmore said, turning right onto Dock Street as he changed the subject. "There might be something there from Zoey or Benjamin today."

"Okay," Lara said. "But I have a pretty lousy memory."

"That's genetics for you."

Mr. Passmore drew out his keys from his pocket and unlocked the back door to the restaurant, which opened onto its cramped kitchen. A large gas range spanned the wall to her right, and pots and pans hung on hooks above it. At the end was a huge, stainless steel refrigerator and a swinging door into the restaurant's dining area.

"I'll chop the vegetables for the omelets," Lara offered, squeezing through. She opened the big fridge and stared inside. "Is Christopher working today?"

"Yep," Mr. Passmore said, glancing at a schedule tacked above the phone. "He'll be in for breakfast, then he's going to tend bar in the afternoon. He's seemed bummed the past few days since Aisha's been gone."

"I'll go easy on him," Lara said.

Mr. Passmore rubbed his hands together. "Okay. I'm going to grind up some coffee beans to get my middle-aged blood going." He stopped suddenly near the reservations book. "Oh, no," he said, picking up a cassette tape. "Zoey forgot her favorite Mariah Carey tape."

Lara turned away and rolled her eyes. Mariah Carey. How completely lame. It was so Zoey Passmore to love Mariah Carey.

"God," Mr. Passmore said, staring at the tape. "I miss her."

Lara bit her lip as she placed three sweet onions on the chopping board. That was one thing she wasn't going to be honest about with her dad. Having Zoey on a different coast was the brightest spot in her existence right now.

He let out a short laugh, then dumped his ground coffee into the coffeemaker. "You're going to have to bear with me, Lara. But I've been dreading this week for a long time."

Lara cleared her throat. "You mean—Zoey living away from home for the first time?"

"Yeah."

Lara ripped off an onion skin, trying to push away the anger she felt rising in her chest like fire. Zoey had absolutely no idea what she had. She was completely oblivious.

"I was more prepared for Benjamin leaving,"

Mr. Passmore went on, staring absently into space. "I'm just so grateful he got his vision back. For Benjamin, leaving for college was a huge victory."

Lara nodded. College was a victory for Benjamin, and she was happy for him, too, although she missed him a lot. Then again, Benjamin didn't make her feel the way Zoey did. Benjamin knew a lot about pain and disappointment. He appreciated what he had.

Lara took a bell pepper and cored it.

Until a few days ago, Zoey's biggest life decision had been deciding which dress to wear to the senior prom. Now she'd have to worry about Lucas and Nina. *It will be good therapy for Zoey*, Lara thought. *I practically did her a favor by exposing her to a real problem.* Actually Lara was beginning to wonder whether that was true. She was beginning to think that telling Zoey about Lucas and Nina had been a huge waste of time.

It had been exciting at first to discover that strong, silent Lucas had actually slipped up, like she herself had a hundred times before. *But the whole messy business had only been a distraction, really*, Lara thought. Sort of like watching a *Baywatch* rerun on TV when what you really wanted was dinner and a movie in town.

Torturing the likes of Zoey Passmore just

wasn't going to cut it anymore. It was time to reach for something bigger. Like maybe putting her portfolio together. She didn't want to go back to where she had been. It was time to move on.

"Okay," Mr. Passmore said briskly, taking his first sip of coffee and checking his watch. "Let's do this." He walked over to the restaurant's front door and turned over the Closed sign. "Did you close up last night, Lara? The place looks great."

"Thanks."

"I'm going to offer an oatmeal special this morning," her father said, pulling a heavy pot off a hook and setting it on the stove. He measured out the water, dumped it in the pot, then pulled a box of matches off the ledge above the gas range.

Lara winced. There was the sound of the gas being turned on. The scratch of the match and the tiny explosion of hot flame at the tip. She watched, transfixed, as her dad touched the match to the stream of invisible gas. The blue flames scrambled around the ring, sending off ribbons of orange and white.

She looked away uneasily, then took a deep, shaky breath.

Nina

Dear Zoey,

This is by far the hardest letter I've ever written to anyone. I've been writing and rewriting this so that it would be perfect, so that it would say everything I want it to say.

But I guess I can never say everything, so I tried to just get down the important stuff.

I don't know what Lara told you. But it doesn't really matter because the truth is this: You are my best friend.

I miss you.

And Lucas is very much in love with you. Believe me.

I am completely ashamed. Please tell me what to do. Because I don't think I could take it if we couldn't be friends anymore. Nobody else is you, Zoey.

Nobody else even comes close.

Love,
Nina

Five

"That's all for our first class," Dr. Langley, Zoey's Twentieth-Century Novel professor, said in conclusion. "I'll cover the first half of Steinbeck's *Grapes of Wrath* on Thursday."

Zoey slapped her notebook shut and looked over the big, amphitheater-style lecture room that sloped down to the lectern. There was a thunderous sound as a hundred wooden writing platforms swung down and two hundred feet stomped toward the door.

"This prof loves to give pop quizzes," a guy next to Zoey murmured. "Thought you'd like to know."

Zoey turned. The guy was olive skinned, with thick, curly brown hair. He was leaning back in his seat, ankles crossed, wearing a baggy shirt over 501 Levis. The room was quickly emptying, and everyone seemed rushed, but this guy acted like he had all the time in the world.

"How do you know?" Zoey asked, standing and stuffing the notebook into her pack.

"I had a premonition," the guy said, standing also and sticking his tiny notebook in his shirt pocket. He flashed Zoey a smile. "Actually, my roommate told me."

"Oh," Zoey said. "Your roommate the know-it-all or your roommate the source of really fantastic information?"

The guy stuck out his hand. "He's a know-it-all, and I'm Kevin Cardeski. Junior. San Francisco native and potential Berkeley dropout."

"Hi, Kevin," Zoey replied, accepting his handshake. Kevin fell into step with Zoey as they headed out of the classroom together.

"Dr. Langley's amazing," Zoey remarked, drinking in the sharp smell of oak, bay, and eucalyptus, which mingled with the scent of the falafel and doughnut stands on the other side of UC Berkeley's main gate. From this high point on the hillside campus she could see straight across the bay, where the Golden Gate Bridge stood in the mist. It was a quantum leap forward from Weymouth High, student body six hundred, with its sweeping views of the local mall and Burger King.

"Yeah, Dr. Langley's one of the best," Kevin agreed. "He's pretty demanding as far as the reading list goes—not to mention a paper every month or so—but his mind is totally wrapped around his subject. The legend is that he and

Steinbeck himself used to hang at the North Beach bars in San Francisco."

"Wow." Zoey's eyes grew wide. "He makes me want to read everything about ten times just so I don't miss anything."

"So," Kevin said, still standing next to her, "are you—what—a junior, senior?"

Zoey eyed him. "I'm a freshman. You flatter me."

"How'd you get into Langley's class? It's for upperclassmen."

Zoey shrugged. Her sandals slapped against the granite steps. "I wanted the class, so I sent in a bunch of references and they waived the no-freshman rule."

"Are you always this confident?" Kevin asked, half serious.

"Actually," Zoey told him, "I'm from a really small town in Maine, so I'm used to pretending that I know what I'm doing, even when I really don't. Especially then."

They turned past the jammed bicycle racks and threaded their way through the crowds toward the squarish, three-story student union that stood on the flat part of the campus. Kiosks fluttered with flyers and notices. A big crowd was gathered around a group of drummers, whose music bonged off the adjacent building walls. Zoey felt pretty good. She loved the sun. She loved the crowd. She loved the change.

"You want to get some coffee?" Kevin asked, breaking into her thoughts.

Zoey hesitated. Kevin seemed nice enough, but she felt like being slightly anonymous and unattached on her first day of classes. So she was relieved when she saw Anika's familiar braid and Serengeti sunglasses flash by on her bike.

"Anika!" Zoey shouted, waving.

She watched as Anika slowed, stopped, then turned to wave, her bronzed shoulders shining in the sunlight.

"We're getting coffee," Zoey yelled. "Wanna come?"

"Okay," Anika called back, raising her leg up over the bike's crossbar, dismounting, then weaving her way through the crowd toward them.

After Zoey made the introductions, she, Anika, and Kevin found an espresso stand, then ended up lounging on the student union steps, staring out over the crowds. Zoey leaned back on her elbows, satisfied. How could she feel so at home in the midst of thousands of total strangers?

"How are we coping with California campus life today?" Anika asked no one in particular, taking a swig of latte.

Zoey spread her arms wide. "I love it." She

hesitated a moment, strangely, as if she wanted to say something in defense of her home, which after all was a kind paradise of its own, even if it had become way too familiar and complicated.

"Must be a bit of a change from Chatham Island," Anika pointed out. "I bet they didn't have soybean curd milk shakes there."

Zoey laughed. "My parents are working on it."

"You lived on an island?" Kevin asked.

"Yeah. In Maine." Anika turned to him. "Didn't she tell you?"

"I thought you talked funny," Kevin teased.

"We do that on purpose," Zoey said with a pang.

"I can picture it now," Anika went on. "No smog. Quaint little towns where everyone leaves their door unlocked. Cute lobster fishermen with bulging muscles."

Zoey felt herself momentarily swept away by the image of Lucas on his father's boat, slicing across the glassy morning waters as the gulls swooped and screamed overhead.

Anika pointed playfully at Zoey, a look of recognition on her face. "She actually *knows* a cute lobster fisherman! I can tell from the faraway look on her face. That is so cool."

Zoey smiled and shook her head. "All the lobster fishermen I know are about a thousand years old and hardly qualify as 'cute,'" she lied. The last thing she wanted to think about was Chatham Island.

"Hey." Kevin sat up. "Did you do any sea kayaking out there in Maine?"

Zoey shrugged. "Once or twice. L.L. Bean land and all."

"Actually she's a surfer girl," Anika broke in. "Hadn't you heard?"

"A bunch of us are heading out to Angel Island the weekend after next to kayak Raccoon Straits and Sausalito," Kevin spoke up. "You guys want to come? We can pick up a couple of rentals."

"Sure," Zoey and Anika said in unison.

"Surfing this weekend," Anika said with mock agony. "Kayaking the weekend after that. And I'm supposed to be putting at least a hundred miles a weekend on my bike this fall."

Zoey nudged her. "Make up for it during the week."

Anika took a final gulp of coffee and tossed her paper cup in the garbage. "I'm heading back to the room to get some writing done. My poetry seminar meets tonight at Professor Paley's house, and I have zilch." She stood up and looked at Zoey. "You coming?"

Zoey stood up, too. "I'm headed that way,

actually. I want to stop by the *Berkeley Bulletin* office and see if they need any writers."

"Wow," Kevin admired. "You don't waste any time."

Zoey grinned. "Maybe they need someone to write about kayaking around Angel Island." She waved. "See you in class, Kevin."

Zoey waved to Anika, too, as she mounted her bike and zoomed off through the crowd. The coffee, the sun on her face, and the thunder of the drums and music made her heart beat fast.

She hiked her pack higher on her shoulder and headed off to the right, in the direction of a building where she'd seen a small sign for the student newspaper offices. She passed a grassy stretch where a group of bare-chested guys were flipping a Frisbee back and forth, then plunged onto a path crowded with bikes and students hurrying out of a massive building. She moved toward them, smiling to herself, not entirely sure if she were moving in the right direction.

And not caring.

Zoey

Dear Benjamin,

So far, things are awfully, awfully good. Sometimes I just cross my fingers and say to myself: Please let this be real because it seems so right. Yes, you were correct about Berkeley: It's not the kind of California you see on TV. It's a city with all the related problems like noisy buses and smog. But I feel so strangely at home, as if I were meant to be here.

I'm going surfing this weekend with my roommate. Hope everything is singing in NYC.

Love,
Zoey

Six

Lara finished wiping down the last of the lunch tables, then dried her hands on her apron. Passmores' had been unexpectedly full for the Wednesday crab cake lunch special, but now only a few stragglers were seated at the bar, staring out at the foggy weather that had enveloped North Harbor since morning. She swept the restaurant floor, took two reservations for the following weekend, filled the dishwasher, and unloaded a delivery of organic lettuce and tomatoes from a local grower.

Lara slipped onto a bar stool and began counting out her tip money as Christopher wiped down a set of beer mugs. "Twenty-one dollars and thirty-five cents in tips," Lara finally said.

"Pretty good shift, huh?" Christopher asked, placing a mug back on the shelf behind him.

"Looks like it," Lara murmured. She stopped and stared at Christopher's back as he turned. She'd never really thought about it, but she admired the way Christopher plugged away at whatever job he could get his hands on—even now that his fiancé, Aisha Gray, had left for Harvard.

"Don't spend it all in one place," Christopher said dryly, twisting a white cloth inside a mug until it sparkled.

Lara shrugged. "I am. I'm spending it all at Lynch Paints. I need more paper and two canvases. Plus, I'm low on charcoal pencils."

Christopher set his rag down hard and looked at her. "What's come over you?"

Lara stared back. "What did you think I was going to spend it on? Tequila?" She regretted the question the minute it was out of her mouth.

Christopher set both broad hands up on the bar, only half smiling. He said nothing.

Lara glared at him. "Well, I'm not. Okay?"

Christopher cocked an eyebrow, which only made her more furious.

"Let me know if you need more money than that," Mr. Passmore said, walking out from the kitchen. "I can advance some of your salary."

"Oh," Lara said, slipping on her leather jacket. She stuffed her hands in her pockets. "Okay." She wasn't used to people offering to loan her money, especially people who had absolutely no reason to trust her. But then, the Passmores weren't your typical kind of adults.

Lara checked her watch and headed out the

side door into the breezy late afternoon. She still had plenty of time to do some drawing before taking the 5:10 ferry into Weymouth for supplies, then returning for the dinner cleanup shift.

"Letter from Benjamin!" she heard Ms. Passmore call out. Lara looked up and saw her heading across the cobblestone street from the direction of the North Harbor post office, waving a white envelope in the air.

Lara stuck her hands in her pockets. "Great."

"And a postcard from Zoey, too!" Ms. Passmore said joyfully.

"Great," Lara said again, more quietly this time.

"Come back in and read them with us, Lara," Ms. Passmore said, waving her back through the door. She ducked her head in the kitchen. "Jeff! Mail from the kids!"

A letter from Zoey, too, Lara thought irritably. She was anxious to hear from Benjamin, but she didn't know if she could stomach a perky postcard from Zoey. She could hear it now:

> *My trip was terrific! I got all the classes I wanted! I already have tons of friends! My roommate is perfect! My life is perfect! And yours is not! Love, Zoey!*

Her father burst out of the kitchen's swinging doors, rubbing his hands together. "Okay.

Let's hear them." He glanced Lara's way. "Come on, Lara. Stay for a minute and listen."

Lara was relieved to see that Ms. Passmore was opening Benjamin's first. The three of them sank down into chairs at the nearest table.

"'Dear Mom, Dad, and Lara,'" Ms. Passmore began, looking tearfully at the page. She glanced over at Mr. Passmore and shook her head. "I still can't get used to the idea that he's gone."

Lara felt an unexpected lump form in her throat. She missed Benjamin, too. Probably more than she was willing to admit.

I'm just writing a brief note to let you know that things are generally okay. My new address is on the back of the envelope, so don't lose it, because I'm expecting you to write and maybe send me a few bucks now and then. Registration went okay. I'm taking Western philosophy, English comp, calculus, and a music theory class. Yeah, the classes are all huge and impersonal, but to make up for this, Columbia has had me surgically inserted into the smallest possible cubicle of a dorm room, where I'm likely to get to know my roommate pretty well. NYC is very cool, of course. And I'll be happy to give you carefully edited accounts of my experiences

when I write to you again next weekend.
Love,
Benjamin

Ms. Passmore folded the letter and smiled tearfully at her husband.

"Let hear what Zoey's got to say," Mr. Passmore said, changing the subject.

Lara sat back in her chair. *Here it comes.*

Ms. Passmore looked at the front of the postcard, which had a color photograph of the Golden Gate Bridge on it. Then she turned it over and smiled. "All it says is: 'Sometimes things are just as beautiful in real life as they are in a touched-up photo. This is one of them, as are you guys. Thanks for everything. Love, Zoey.'"

Lara watched uncomfortably as Ms. Passmore pushed her hand into Mr. Passmore's, still staring at the postcard, her eyes damp. Mr. Passmore shook his head wordlessly, then, to Lara's surprise, slipped his hand into her own.

"We're glad you're with us, Lara," her father said. "Just having you around is a great help."

Lara shrugged. "Thanks," she croaked as she got up. The room felt suddenly hot, and there was the faint smell of gas that annoyed her. She wasn't used to it, she told herself, since her mother had always cooked on tiny electric stoves or hot plates in their broken-down apartments.

Still, watching the flames from the range flare up as they did had begun to irritate her. Maybe even upset her.

But Lara was determined not to let it.

She squeezed her father's hand briefly and without a word hurried out the door toward the ferry dock.

Seven

Dear Zoey, Nina began.

"Nina!"

"Yeah?"

"Dinner!"

"I'm not hungry."

There was silence at the other side of the door.

Nina lay there on her bed, waiting for the sound of her stepmother's little mouse footsteps to disappear down the carpeted hall. All Nina needed now was the creak of the top step—a long-standing Geiger household signal that the intruder was giving up.

There it was. The creak. The stepmother was gone.

Nina stared up at the Pearl Jam poster on her ceiling. A blurry photograph of a sheep baring its teeth in a big grin. She wasn't sure why she put it up, except that it sort of represented the way she saw life looking at her these days. The sheep as Fate—smirking at her.

More footsteps up the stairs and down the hall. Heavier. Her father's.

"Nina?"

"Yes?"

"May I come in?"

"No."

"I'm coming in, Nina."

Nina watched the door open and her father enter. He closed the door softly behind him, then picked his way carefully over the clothes, magazines, candy wrappers, and balled-up paper wads that littered her floor. Burke Geiger was a tall man, with wavy white hair and big hands that he liked to clasp in front of him when he was talking. Nina crossed her arms over her chest as he sat down on the edge of the bed.

"Everything go okay at school today?"

Nina rolled her eyes. "Oh, yeah. Loved it."

"I know it must be tough with all your friends gone," her father began. "And your sister, too."

"I don't miss my sister."

Her father smiled. "I see. You needed a break from Claire, huh?"

"You could put it that way."

Her dad patted her leg. "She called home about half an hour ago."

Nina stared. "You're kidding. She's been gone less than a week."

Mr. Geiger nodded knowingly. "Yes. If you ask me, Claire is missing Chatham Island a bit."

"That's ridiculous," Nina objected. "She couldn't wait to be on her own."

Mr. Geiger stared at the ceiling. "She wanted us to send her a few things."

"Like what?" Nina wanted to know. "Her broomstick?"

"Some photographs . . ."

Nina's jaw dropped. "Of *us?*" she asked, shocked.

"Oh, yes. And a book or two she forgot. And her old pillow. It seems the new pillow is too strange."

"Whew."

Mr. Geiger drew his salt-and-pepper eyebrows together. "Won't you come down? Sarah's made a roast turkey and an enormous chocolate cake."

Nina looked at her dad and felt a little sorry for him. He meant well, but did he actually think that turkey and chocolate cake could help her at a time like this? Not that he knew anything about what was upsetting her, of course, since she hadn't told him. But—couldn't he *tell?*

"Maybe in a few minutes, Dad, okay?" Nina said.

"Heard from Zoey?" he asked.

Nina softened even more. He really didn't

have a clue, did he? It really wasn't his fault, but how could she possibly explain what had happened with her and Zoey and Lucas?

"No," Nina said quietly. "Not yet. I got a postcard from Benjamin, though, and he loves New York."

Mr. Geiger patted her again and stood up. "You've got good friends, Nina. Hang on to them."

Tears began to flood Nina's eyes just as her father turned and headed for the door.

"Sorry, I'm busy tonight," Claire cheerfully told the guy from her calculus class. She hurried down the wide flight of stairs that opened out into a lobby, crammed with students hurrying to classes and professors emerging from faculty rooms.

"Maybe we could just go for coffee?" the guy asked, jogging lightly across the polished floor to keep up with her. He was very tall and wore a short-sleeved button-down shirt tucked into plaid shorts.

Claire gripped the leather strap of her book bag and with her other hand pushed open the glass door that led outside to the main campus quad. She paused to take in the crisp air and the late afternoon sun lighting up the brick buildings across MIT's central quad.

"Coffee?" the guy repeated, still next to her.

Claire was used to guys asking her out on the spot, but now every strange guy reminded her of her last few horrible weeks in North Harbor. The weeks in which she had been stalked by a psychopathic guy she barely knew.

She gritted her teeth. Once upon a time, Claire had made a friend over the Internet—Sean. They had become close; that is, they were close until Claire saw him in person. Claire saw him and rejected him because he was too heavy. Apparently this had sent Sean over the edge. He lost close to two hundred pounds and then came after Claire. He looked so different that he was able to get very close to her—without her ever knowing it. Luckily Claire had put the pieces together in time to rescue Benjamin just as he was about to become Sean's first official victim—punishment for having received a kiss on the cheek from Claire.

Ever since then she'd been wary of strangers—especially male ones.

Although she was determined to make a fresh start at MIT, Claire decided it didn't have to be with the geek who was pursuing her now.

"I'm sorry," Claire said politely, looking hard into his eyes, which were framed by square black glasses. "But—no."

The guy took two steps back before turning

around and walking away. Claire smiled and walked in the opposite direction. The route she took back to her dorm followed the glassy-smooth Charles River, past several athletic fields and a grassy amphitheater. She walked briskly past the scattered students reading in the sun. Bicycles whizzed by her on the path to Barron Hall.

"Claire!"

Claire stopped, then turned her head slightly. Out of the blur of strange faces a familiar one emerged.

"Jake?" Claire half whispered, walking toward the steps where he was sitting.

"Hi," Jake said, standing up.

An unfamiliar feeling washed over Claire, and she smiled with genuine pleasure at him. "What are you doing here?" she asked.

Jake shrugged. "Just stopping by."

"Mmm-hmm." Claire stared at him. "Why are you *really* here, Jake?" She sat down next to him on the bench he had occupied, wrapped her arms around her books, and looked at him suspiciously.

He looked about the same, she thought. But it was different now that they were both off island—she at MIT and Jake at Boston University. On the island she looked *through* people because she'd already seen them a thousand times before.

Here she took them in. And now she saw that Jake had the same clean-cut face, short dark hair, and phenomenal torso as always. She was suddenly surprised at how good it was to see him again.

Jake rubbed the back of his neck. "I don't know, Claire. I thought you might be able to help me out."

Claire frowned slightly, wondering what in the world he wanted.

"I remembered you said you were staying at Barron Hall," Jake said, making conversation.

"Good memory," Claire said warily.

Jake seemed uncomfortable. He crossed his arms tightly across his chest and gave her a long look. "Claire. Can we talk?"

She stood up and nodded toward the door. "Sure. Want to see my room? It's huge."

"Yeah. I would."

Claire wasn't sure what Jake was up to, but she didn't really care.

"How's your roommate?" Jake asked her as they wove their way through the crowd in the lobby. He punched the elevator button for her.

"Sixth floor," Claire said as the door opened. "My roommate is perfect in every way."

"What?" Jake grinned at her. "She must be awesome if you haven't tried to kill her yet—or if she hasn't tried to kill you. You were voted Most

Impossible by the student body, remember?"

"Ha, ha," she said without a trace of humor. "You're a laugh a minute, Jake." Claire nudged him, then let him follow her out of the elevator and down the hall to her room. "For your information," she said as she unlocked the door and swung it open, "I don't have a roommate."

Jake walked over to the window, then shook his head. "How much extra did Burke have to pay for this cushy situation?"

Claire shrugged. "Nothing. I think the housing people decided I wasn't fit to share space with another human being."

Jake raised his eyebrows. "Smart move."

Claire curled up on the corner of her bed, which was decorated with a fluffy down comforter, several large pillows, and a small stuffed leopard. "Have you talked to Kate?"

Jake shook his head and sat down on the opposite bed. "Not yet. I feel weird about calling her mom's house. She never liked me much."

"It's strange how everyone left the island at once," Claire said. But she guessed that Kate didn't want to stay there without Jake, so moving back to New York with her mother must have made sense at the time.

"Yeah." Jake paused. "I saw Aisha."

Claire smiled and fell back on her pillows. "How does she like Harvard? She must be pretty happy, at least when she's not thinking about Christopher."

"Actually, she's got a pretty obnoxious roommate," Jake said. "She looked miserable to me. Hey, speaking of miserable, where's Aaron Mendel these days?"

Claire was stunned for a moment. *Aaron?* She hadn't thought about her boyfriend in a very long time. Not since he had called to ask about the stalker and had made it sound as though Claire was making a huge issue out of nothing. Where was he? She racked her brain for the answer. "He's . . . in Chicago. He's got a big engagement there for another couple of weeks—his band has a gig there."

"Huh," Jake said absently, looking out the window.

"So what about *your* roommate, Jake? You haven't told me what the deal is."

Jake pulled out one of Claire's desk chairs and sat down in it backward, leaning his chin over his folded arms. "I don't have a roommate, Claire. I don't even have a room."

"Bingo," Claire said instantly. "That's what this is all about."

Jake rubbed his eyes. "The BU housing people screwed up. Some idiot looked at my housing application and read it as *Jane* McRoyan instead of Jake."

Claire's jaw dropped. "They assigned you to a woman's room?"

Jake nodded, his dark eyes burning. "Yeah. Well, you may think it's funny, Claire, but it wasn't so funny when I walked into the room and this—well, this really unattractive woman was standing there with nothing but a towel wrapped around her head."

"Oh, Jake," she said, trying not to laugh. "That's so—" She was going to say "horrible." But Jake looked so serious, and she was trying so hard to suppress her giggles that all she could do was snort, which only made her dissolve into laughter.

"It turns out that Spaulding Hall is an all-women's dorm. I didn't even realize it until my 'roommate' told me."

"So," Claire said, attempting to calm down, "she got to keep the room, and you got thrown out?"

Jake nodded.

"That's discrimination!" Claire practically shouted, then fell into another fit of giggles. "You should sue!"

"Now who's a laugh a minute?" Jake asked. "The worst part is that the housing people have nothing," he went on, burying his face in his arms. "There's nothing for rent in Cambridge under a thousand a month. My stuff is in storage, I have no place to live, I've been staying at an incredibly scrungy youth hostel, and my first class is tomorrow."

Suddenly Claire stopped laughing. She stared at him.

Jake looked up at her with pleading eyes.

"Jake," Claire warned.

"Please, Claire."

Claire's mouth dropped open. "Are you kidding? I couldn't let you stay here even if I *did* take pity on you. It's strictly against the rules. I could lose this room."

"Just for a few days," Jake begged. "Something's got to come up. What am I going to do, Claire? Go back to Chatham Island?"

Claire gave Jake a horrified look. "God."

"Claire . . ."

Claire leaned her head back on her pillow, then lifted up her right hand and stared at her nails. Jake, after all, was a totally honorable, follow-the-rules-and-you'll-get-ahead guy. It was unthinkable that Jake McRoyan could be lying to her or have any ulterior motive whatsoever. So why shouldn't she help him?

"I don't know, Jake," Claire said carefully. "I don't like the idea of getting kicked out."

Jake's eyes were filled with sincerity. "I'll leave before six each morning. And your room is right next to the stairway. I'd only be visible in the hall for about five seconds."

Claire tapped her chin with one glossy nail. "That's true."

Jake stared down at the floor.

"Let me get one thing straight," Claire said slowly. "I want complete quiet. I don't want you in here before nine P.M. No noise. No problems."

"Thank you, Claire."

"And one other thing."

"Yes?"

"You're going to owe me. Big time."

Lara

I think I should write this dream down, even though the only thing I have to write in is one ob Zoey's old history notebooks. She'll probably have a tantrum when she binds the missing page.

Anyway in my dream I was standing in a wide open bield in bront ob my easel, painting a picture ob the pines at the top ob a ridge. I was using oils, and I remember how smoothly and beautibully the green shades spread on the canvas. It was almost like there was no paint between me and

the scene I was painting. Just my
thoughts and then the picture.

I was halfway through the painting
when the air began to smell like smoke.
I looked over my shoulder and saw
that a grass fire was spreading quickly
up the hill I was standing on.

I was really panicked, so I grabbed my
wet canvas and began running up the hill
toward the pine forest. The smoke scorched
my nose and my lungs and was moving
so fast that I figured my only escape
was up into one of the trees ahead.

I had to drop my painting as I
grabbed a scratchy pine branch and began
climbing as quickly as I could. I was
pretty relieved when I realized the tree

was actually beginning to grow while I climbed, stretching up toward the sky as if it were alive and trying to rescue me.

At that point I looked down and saw that Jeff and Darla had run up the hill too, but since the tree had grown, the bottom branches were too high for them to reach.

As I watched, totally scared and helpless, the fire quickly reached the base of the tree where Jeff and Darla were standing. A burning, smoking cloud sort of washed over them, and we all started screaming: me, my father, and Darla, until I could not tell whose cry I was hearing. . . .

And then I woke up.

Eight

Lara zipped up the front of her leather jacket and took one last swig of cold ferry coffee. The boat had already docked in Weymouth, but her eyes had been so heavy from lack of sleep, she had to give herself a moment to pry them open.

She felt for the handle of her cardboard portfolio, pressing her lips into a nervous line. Breakfast had been an impossibility; her stomach was a wreck. And now she felt sick, regretting miserably the phone call she'd made to Sandy Krukmeyer the night before.

Five minutes of crazed confidence and I make an appointment with her.

Now all Lara wanted to do was stay on the ferry and make the trip back to Chatham Island without getting off. Instead she stood up shakily and headed for the gangway. Once outside she sucked in the fresh air and hurried down Fourth Avenue toward the Weymouth commons. Sandy Krukmeyer's gallery stood across from the grassy central square. It had a neatly painted, white storefront with large gold lettering over the door that read S&K.

It had been only a week since her brief talk with Sandy at the backyard barbecue, but since then Lara had been drawing every spare minute.

Lara opened the door and walked cautiously into the gallery's empty, echoing space. A collection of large watercolors covered both walls, and a well-dressed couple stood in front of one of them, staring.

She proceeded, terrified, across the glossy wood floor toward a door in the back, where she found Sandy just hanging up the telephone.

"Hi," Lara said, heart sinking. She had a sudden, overwhelming thought that Sandy wanted to see her work out of charity or out of pity for Jeff Passmore's troubled teenager.

"Hi," Sandy said, distracted and serious. A pair of black glasses hung on a beaded strand around her neck. She glanced at Lara's portfolio case. "Good. It looks like you brought lots of stuff for me."

"Yes."

Sandy brushed the hair off her forehead with the back of her wrist. "It may be quiet around here right now, but just wait until the weekend. We're getting ready for a showing of Craig Hillman photographs. It's arriving from Boston this afternoon. We're going to have to work fast to set up."

"Oh."

Sandy walked quickly out onto the main floor, pointing to an opening into another room on the left. "You've been in here, Lara. We like to show our local artists in this more intimate area, and we have a lot of wonderful work. Right now I've got some raku pottery made by a young man in Rockland."

Lara followed, staring at the pottery and sculpture displayed on white, rectangular columns and shelves. He had used some incredible metallic glazes, and the whole display seemed to shimmer in the sunshine that streamed in through the skylights.

"Okay," Sandy said in a businesslike manner. She swept her hand toward a table she had set up. "What did you bring me?"

"Um, some pastels," Lara said hesitantly. Her work seemed hopelessly boring compared to the incredible things that surrounded her.

Lara nervously unwound the string on her portfolio case, wishing she could turn around and run back to the ferry.

"So you're working with charcoal, and some oil, and now pastels, too?" Sandy asked. "Pretty versatile."

Lara shrugged. "Well, you haven't seen them yet."

Sandy said nothing. She sat down and slipped on her glasses.

One by one Lara drew out the pastels she had done. They were mostly portraits—some men, some women—loosely based on the faces of people from her old neighborhood in Boston. Faces torn with anger, or despair, or madness. Faces she hadn't been able to shake from her mind—that reminded her of what she'd walked away from, almost without realizing it, when she came to Chatham Island.

All the pictures had been done quickly, almost maniacally, late at night with a set of pastels she'd bought as an afterthought the week before.

Lara placed six of them neatly in a row, then stood back uncomfortably as Sandy looked at them.

A few long moments passed. Sandy touched one of the portraits lightly at its bottom corner.

Lara cleared her throat. "I—I just wanted to do a little experimenting," she stammered, zipping her jacket up and down. "The pastels are kind of fun for doing a quick drawing." *Oh, my God, she hates them,* she thought. *What am I doing here? I must have been insane to come—*

Sandy turned to look at her. "Experimenting? You mean you'd never worked with pastels before this?"

Lara looked back. "Um. Well, I did a few times in high school. I took an art class once."

Sandy looked down again at Lara's faces. "You've chosen tones that work extremely well for these subjects. They're delicate, and yet the expressions are almost violent—the juxtaposition makes them incredibly compelling."

"Thanks," Lara said, although she wasn't sure what *juxtaposition* meant.

Sandy shook her head. "Pastels are very difficult."

Lara shrugged. "I like them. It's fun because, well, it's kind of dangerous. Once you put the color to the paper, there's no going back. So I worked sort of quickly. I just wanted to get a feeling down without worrying about the details."

Sandy bit her thumbnail. "They're very good." She looked at Lara again. "Can you do more?"

Lara's heart sped up. "Yes."

"I wasn't going to tell you this right away, but I can't help myself," Sandy went on. "Each year I sponsor at least two young artists at the Eastern Seaboard Harvest Festival, which is in about a month. If you can put together a half dozen or so pieces more like these and I like them, I'll sponsor you."

Lara stared. "What does that mean—you'll sponsor me?"

"It means I'll pay to have your work framed and invite you to be a part of the show," Sandy explained. "I often make quite a few sales during festival time, so you might even sell a picture or two."

Lara paused. It took her a moment to realize that Sandy was being completely straight with her—this well-dressed, successful, grown woman who wasn't a relation or a social worker. Lara's own dyed hair, funky jacket, and totally obvious insecurity apparently weren't a factor. She was actually being taken seriously. Sandy Krukmeyer of S&K Gallery was taking her *artwork* seriously.

"So," Sandy said, smiling, "what do you think? Can you fit it into your work schedule? Will your dad give you enough time off from the restaurant over the next few days to give me your very best work?"

"Yes," Lara whispered. "I mean, *yes*," she said in a louder voice. "I—guess so. I mean, I don't know."

"Don't know what?"

"I don't know—if I'm good enough. I mean, I'm just a beginner," Lara stuttered.

"Maybe it's the fact that you're new to art that makes your work so fresh. You just get yourself back home and get to work. But before you take off, let me seal those pastels for you before something happens to them, okay?"

Lara nodded wordlessly, not knowing whether to laugh or to shake with fear. The whole feeling was so confusing and weird, one second she wanted to drink a fifth of vodka and the next climb a mountain.

It was going to take a while to adjust.

"Hello?" Aisha said into the receiver, already grabbing a pencil to take down a message for Felicia. People were always calling for her roommate, and it was starting to get annoying. Aisha probably wouldn't have minded so much if most of Felicia's friends weren't so rude.

"Aisha, hi."

There was a pause, and Aisha wondered why people expected you to recognize their voices. She'd only been at school for a week, for goodness' sake—was she supposed to be able to identify every caller by the way he or she said her name?

"Yes, this is Aisha," she hinted, hoping that the caller would identify herself. It was a woman, that much Aisha knew.

"So formal! Aisha, it's Claire."

Aisha nearly dropped the receiver.

"Claire?" she asked. Since she couldn't think of any reason that Claire would be calling her, she added, "Is everything okay?"

There was a pause, then, "Of course everything's okay. Everything's great! I'm just . . . I'm just calling to see how you're doing." *There was something strange about Claire's voice,* Aisha thought. In fact, this entire phone call was moderately peculiar.

"Um, I'm fine," Aisha said, not exactly eager to confide anything to Claire.

"I hear from Jake you're not exactly wild about your roommate," Claire went on.

"She's okay," Aisha replied. "It's just hard sharing a space. You know how it is."

"Actually," Claire said, "I'm beginning to find out." Aisha wondered briefly what that meant, but Claire went on. "Anyway, I was thinking that you and I should get together sometime. We live awfully close. We could compare notes on the joy of being totally anonymous."

"Um, sure. Let's do that," Aisha said, somewhat bewildered. Claire had never sought her out before. What was going on? "Do you want to give me a call next week, when I have a better idea of what my schedule is? We could have lunch or coffee or something."

"Oh," Claire said. "Sure."

Was it Aisha's imagination, or did Claire sound *disappointed*? What did she expect, that Aisha would drop everything and run over to MIT right *now*?

Aisha decided not to worry about it. "Great," she said, "then I'll talk to you soon."

"Okay," Claire replied. "Next week, then. Bye."

"Bye, Claire. Thanks for calling."

Aisha hung up. "How odd," she muttered to herself. If Aisha didn't know better, she would almost have said that Claire sounded . . . home-sick.

"Shhh."

"I'm sorry, Claire," Jake whispered. "I just don't know if I can do this."

Claire looked at him irritably. It was six-thirty Friday morning, and she was preparing Jake for his departure down the Barron Hall fire escape, a concrete stairwell whose entrance was approximately ten steps from Claire's dorm-room door at the end of the hall. Though it was unlikely that any one of the thirty doors along the hallway would open at the exact instant Jake bolted for the fire escape, Claire wasn't willing to take the chance.

If the dorm authorities found out she was harboring a male, her fantastic room situation was doomed.

Which was why Jake was now standing before Claire, bundled into a large, pink-flowered bathrobe she had purchased for three dollars at a thrift shop the afternoon before. His head was enclosed in a frilly shower cap, and to complete Claire's meticulous efforts, his size-eleven feet were squeezed into rose-colored slippers, each one topped with a worn satin bow that bobbed back and forth as he walked.

"Aren't you taking this thing a little too far?" Jake asked.

Claire took Jake by the hand and led him past the rumpled extra bed, where she'd allowed him to sleep the night before. Then she opened the drapes and made him look out at the view of the Charles River. "This is what I'm protecting, Jake. My view. My privacy. My enjoyment of college life. I want to help you, but I don't want you to screw this up for me. Just follow my instructions and everything will work out."

"Got it," Jake said sheepishly, retying his bathrobe belt.

"Now," Claire said firmly, handing him a large quilted shoulder purse covered with pictures of kittens. "Put this over your shoulder. . . ."

"Claire . . ."

"Over your shoulder," Claire repeated, looping it under his arm, then drawing the strap over his massively developed football shoulder. She stood back and studied the effect. "Walk casually to the fire escape door and don't look back down the hall. When you get to the bottom of the stairwell, you will find, conveniently, an unlocked broom closet. Go inside the broom closet, take off your disguise, stuff it inside your purse, and leave the purse behind the big stack of cardboard boxes. I'll pick it up after you're gone."

"Okay," Jake said, biting his lower lip.

"Now go," Claire ordered, steering him toward the door. "And don't forget my instructions."

"Thanks, Claire," Jake whispered. "See you tonight at nine."

Claire smiled at him, enjoying the effect. "You really are beautiful. You know that, don't you?"

"It's a wonderful feeling," Jake said with a sigh.

Nine

"So it follows that if the bodies have a relative orbit with a semimajor axis a, their period of mutual revolution, P, is related to a. . ."

Benjamin squinted at the figures his calculus professor scribbled on the overhead. He'd already been through Newton's derivation of Kepler's law in senior calculus and thought it was pretty straightforward stuff.

He leaned back in his wooden lecture hall chair and thought about his sister, Zoey. He smiled. Zoey would get so bent out of shape that calculus came easily to him. He used to love it when she'd come crawling in on hands and knees before a calculus exam, begging for help.

Have mercy, Zoey would cry, knocking slowly on the other side of his bedroom door, only halfway serious. She always aced those exams, anyway.

Benjamin was enjoying this happy memory when he looked up again casually at his professor's next projection on the large screen in front of him.

He blinked, then blinked again. His left eye. Something was messed up. It was the little black hood again. Over his left eye.

Great. Here we go again, Benjamin thought. The same thing had happened to him—when? Thursday? He'd passed it off as a tiny blip in his eye machinery. His eyes, after all, *had* been through a lot. Complete retinal detachment damage. Major surgery. Why panic over a few crazy spots and shadowy apparitions?

While the professor droned on, Benjamin sat very still, staring straight ahead, waiting for the black curtain to disappear. For a moment he tried to visualize perfect sight: pure color, rays of light bouncing off water. Ever since he'd regained his sight, he'd had this superstition that thinking and acting positively would somehow keep it from slipping away again.

"Newton derived this equation not only for planets moving about the sun but also for any pair of mutually revolving bodies . . . ," his professor continued, scribbling a second equation onto the overhead.

This is not happening, Benjamin told himself, holding still, then blinking.

But the darkness at the top of his vision didn't go away. The equation was impossible for him to see unless he tilted his head way back.

A stabbing pain shot through both of his eyes. He drew his hands up to his face to shut out the light. He wanted to get up and leave, but he made himself stay. He closed his eyes and listened in the dark, just like he had for seven years. Listening in the dark. Always listening.

"Excuse me?" he heard his professor say suddenly in a sharp tone of voice.

Benjamin sat in darkness, waiting for the pain to pass. He wasn't quite sure who the professor was speaking to or why. But he'd used his own super-blind-boy skills since he'd closed his eyes, his mind taking in what had been said, barely forgetting a word.

It was amazing what you could notice and remember when the mind wasn't distracted by details like vision, Benjamin always thought.

"You, over there, sir," the professor repeated. "I'm afraid you've gone and fallen asleep on us. Pardon me for waking you."

Benjamin pulled his eyelids open briefly, realizing that his calculus professor had called on him. Then he closed them again against the painful light. "I'm not asleep, sir."

Benjamin could heard tittering throughout the huge lecture hall.

"Aha!" his professor cried. "I see. You were not sleeping. Well, that's good because these first few lectures of the year are the most important ones I shall give."

Benjamin took a deep breath and let it out slowly. It was clear the guy was just a wee bit sensitive about the slumping masses of cool youth entering his freshman calc classes.

"I would like to point out, Mr. . . . ?"

Benjamin kept his eyes shut. "Passmore."

"Mr. Passmore," the professor continued in a slightly acidic tone, "that I do not consider my classes to be entertainment for you to consume and enjoy while you are moving through your college years. The material we cover is challenging and important. Miss out on the fundamentals we cover in the first few classes and you will be lost, Mr. Passmore. Lost for the remainder of the year! Do I make myself clear?"

"Yes," Benjamin said.

"Now," the professor said calmly. "I'd like you to help me review for the class what we've covered so far today. Please, Mr. Passmore, if you will, state Newton's law of universal gravitation?"

A ripple of amused laughter ran through the lecture hall.

"Newton's law states," Benjamin began, "that between any two objects anywhere in space there exists a force of attraction that is in proportion to the product of the masses of the objects and in inverse proportion to the square of the distance between them." Then he added, "Sir."

There was a heavy silence in the room.

He heard the professor clear his throat. "That is correct," he said quietly, and resumed his lecture.

Once class was over, Benjamin walked slowly out of the lecture hall onto a tree-lined path that led toward his dorm. Slowly, mercifully, the light expanded slightly in his left eye. But he wasn't sure anymore how long it would last.

"You had a call five minutes ago," his roommate told him when he got back to his room. He was listening to jazz and reading the Arts and Leisure section of last Sunday's *New York Times*. "Some guy named Brennan."

"Dr. Brennan," Benjamin murmured. *The ophthalmologist at Mount Sinai Hospital.*

Tom looked up from his paper with a pained expression. "Guess so. Do they have voice mail and call forwarding up there in Maine or wherever you're from? We might want to consider it."

"Did you take down his number?"

Tom jerked his head toward Benjamin's desk. "It's right there."

"Thanks," Benjamin said, taking the phone and lying down on the bed.

"By the way," Tom continued. "You said

you liked to take pictures. I'm reading here that the Whitney Museum has a showing of vintage boxing photographs opening this weekend."

"Mmmm," Benjamin said, punching the number of the Manhattan ophthalmologist Dr. Martin had referred him to. Benjamin had been trying to get an appointment since yesterday morning. He'd had to cancel his first one.

"The Whitney?" Tom asked. "Have you heard of it?"

Benjamin listened as the phone rang.

"Dr. Brennan's office."

"Benjamin Passmore, returning your call."

"Oh, yes, Benjamin," a receptionist said. "You were a referral from Dr. Martin at Boston General. Dr. Brennan has had a cancellation, and we can fit you in at three-thirty if you're available."

Benjamin squinted at his clock. "That's in . . ."

"About forty-five minutes. Shall I pencil you in?"

"Yes," Benjamin said quickly. "I'll be there."

It took the last of Benjamin's spare cash to take a taxi to Mount Sinai, but when he got there, he was relieved he'd done it.

Benjamin waited in the reception area. His eyes were still closed, but his ears were unable to tune out the office's tinny version of the Brandenburg Concertos. A few minutes later he was in Dr. Brennan's chair and someone was putting drops into his eyes.

"I'm glad you got in touch with us," Dr. Brennan said. "Dr. Martin's office just faxed pertinent sections of your file to me," he explained, flipping through a few pages. There was a long silence as Dr. Brennan read through the file, then examined Benjamin's eyes with several different pieces of equipment.

"You had your surgery . . . around the beginning of the year, I see," Dr. Brennan murmured. "Severe macular degeneration. Mmm. I assume you've had regular follow-up visits with Dr. Martin and a minimum of physical activity."

"Not exactly."

Dr. Brennan narrowed his eyes. "Didn't Dr. Martin warn you about the consequences of—"

"Yeah," Benjamin snapped, staring at the ceiling. "He did." Back then Benjamin had been surfing his brains out, bathing himself in sunlight, and reading everything he could get his hands on. The last thing he wanted to do was take it easy. How many people would have had that kind of restraint if their world had been pitch-black for seven years and was suddenly filled with color and light?

"I'll be honest," Dr. Brennan finally said. "I don't like what's going on with your vision."

"That was exactly my reaction," Benjamin

said, his anger rising. He wasn't interested in hearing anything other than that he would get better.

"Look, Benjamin," Dr. Brennan said calmly. "I'm going to recommend that you make an appointment with Dr. Martin. You have a unique and delicate condition, and it's important that the original attending ophthalmologist examine you. Dr. Martin specializes in this problem, and Boston General is far better equipped than this hospital to treat you."

"How am I supposed to do that?" Benjamin demanded. "You want me to make an appointment two hundred miles away when I'm carrying an eighteen-credit load at Columbia and I barely have enough money to live?"

Dr. Brennan looked Benjamin squarely in the face. "I wish I had better news," he said sincerely.

Benjamin clenched his teeth. *Why am I acting this way?* he wondered. *I've been a real jerk ever since I got to New York. I don't have any right to be angry anymore—everything that's happening right now is my own fault.*

"It seems to me, Benjamin, that there are frequent trains that run between New York and Boston. And it seems to me that going to see Dr. Martin would be worth the time and money if the cost of not going is your vision. Of course, that's your decision."

Benjamin thought for a moment. But really, what choice did he have? "Okay," he said. "I'll do it."

"Listen to me, Benjamin," Dr. Brennan said firmly. "If the retina is beginning to detach, you're going to have to take it easy. I want that train ride to be the most vibration your eyes get between now and when Dr. Martin sees you."

"I swear, Anika, I don't have any classes this afternoon," Zoey insisted. "I'm glad we're going early." She swung her pack into the back of Anika's beat-up Vanagon.

"I believe you, I believe you," Anika muttered, digging for her keys. "I don't know if you're capable of cutting a class. For me it's a part of life. Aha!" She held the keys aloft triumphantly. "Besides." She grinned widely. "Surf's up in Santa Cruz."

Zoey gave her the thumbs-up sign.

Anika backed her van out of the dorm's basement garage, then pulled out onto the narrow Berkeley street. She wore a faded Hawaiian shirt over a racing suit, ripped jeans, and running shoes. Zoey wore cutoffs, a new sleeveless T-shirt, and a Red Sox cap.

"If we can beat rush hour over the Bay Bridge, it'll be easy to get on 280 South to Highway 17," Anika explained, driving past

People's Park, then left on Telegraph Avenue toward the interstate.

Zoey rolled down the window. The air smelled of exhaust and sandalwood. Futon shops were crammed next to mountaineering supply stores, coffeehouses, and bookstores. People didn't hurry down Telegraph Avenue, Zoey realized, they strolled—slowly—as if they were sunning themselves at the same time.

Anika dropped her windshield visor down against the afternoon sun. "Highway 17 takes us over the coastal mountains and down into Santa Cruz."

"Great," Zoey said, putting her feet up on the dashboard. "Then I'll get my first look at the Pacific Ocean."

Anika gasped. "You're kidding. God, that's so bizarre. I can't imagine living this long without ever seeing the Pacific."

"Give me a break. I've spent my whole life staring at the ocean," Zoey insisted. "Have you seen the Atlantic?"

Anika shrugged. "Sort of. Does New York Harbor qualify?"

"No."

"Then I guess you win."

Zoey leaned forward as they approached the steel gray Bay Bridge, which stretched from the east bay across to the city of San Francisco, anchored by an island in the middle. In the distance she could see the compact San Francisco waterfront and the city's hills of white buildings beyond. Ahead and to the right she could see the bright red span of the Golden Gate Bridge. "It's beautiful." Zoey sighed.

"I know," Anika agreed. "When I go over this spot, I think that same thing."

Zoey looked over.

"This is where the bridge cracked in two during the '89 earthquake. So this is the last thing that poor driver saw before his car dove straight off the edge into the bay."

Zoey drew her hands to her face. "Oh, my God."

"Great last view, huh?" Anika said.

Zoey laughed. "Gee, what a—what a life-affirming story, Anika."

"Wait until you meet my brother. He's worse than I am. He's adopted, so we don't really know where he came from, but my guess is Jupiter."

Zoey raised her eyebrows. "And where did you say you were from again?" she teased.

"Suburbia. We were both desperate to get out," Anika added. "So I ended up living in the city, and he's going to UC Santa Cruz, which is basically a small beach town. He surfs all the time. He's even writing a book about it."

The road zoomed into San Francisco, then merged onto a wide freeway that headed south through houses and apartments packed onto the sides of rolling hills. They drove in silence for a while, then turned west onto a highway that headed up the coastal range.

Zoey wondered what Benjamin would have thought of this wonderful, sunny place. What was he doing burying himself in crowded, crime-ridden Manhattan when he could have spread his wings out here? Her thoughts turned to Nina, but she stopped herself, and an unexpected flood of emotion nearly flattened her against the seat of the van.

Anika looked over. "Don't look now, but shadows are beginning to form under your eyes. You're not nervous about surfing, are you?"

Zoey looked down at her thumbnail. "No, I—" she started, but stopped herself. Did she really want to tell Anika her sad stories? Zoey wasn't sure. She liked Anika a lot, but there was a major difference between knowing someone for seven days and knowing them for seven years. Or longer. Anika didn't really know the situation or Zoey well enough to understand. Besides, who wanted to think about sad things on such a beautiful day? "Well," Zoey began again, "I guess I am a little nervous, since your brother is practically a pro and I'm such a beginner and everything."

"Don't worry about it," Anika said with a wave of her hand. "He might be a good surfer, but he doesn't expect everyone else to be." She flashed Zoey a reassuring smile. "So did you ever find the *Bulletin* offices?" she asked. "I forgot to ask you."

"You were lost in a poem," Zoey reminded her.

Anika laughed. "Yeah. Then I went to Dr. Paley's house for our very intimate seminar, and everyone ripped it."

Zoey stared. "That's awful."

"Oh, well. That's why I surf and ride my bike. It helps me shake off the bad reviews," Anika explained, shifting down as the van neared the highway's summit. "Plus it was the first seminar. Everyone was marking their territory like little terriers, wanting to get Dr. Paley's attention with their biting remarks. How smart can you look complimenting someone on their poem?"

Zoey shook her head, then brightened. "Yes, I did find the *Bulletin* offices." She dug into a box of crackers and ate one. "Of course it's totally staffed, but I talked to one of the feature editors for about five seconds."

"Really?"

"She said they're always looking for great freelance pieces."

"About what?"

Zoey laughed. "She said she'd know when she saw it. Helpful, huh? I'm going to write about surfing. Or maybe I'll write about non-stop sun. I don't know; it will come to me." Zoey crunched down on a saltine so hard that half of it ended up all over her shirt.

"There's your subject." Anika interrupted Zoey's desperate attempts to shake off the crumbs. "Look: the Pacific."

Zoey looked up. The Pacific Ocean. Smooth and blue and shining. It was amazing how large it seemed and how it curved beautifully away on the horizon like a picture of the earth from space. Zoey wanted nothing more than to plunge herself into and be consumed by it.

"Ten minutes and we'll be there," Anika said, stepping on the accelerator. "I told Peter to have two surfboards waxed and waiting for us. I've got the wet suits in the back. And believe me, we'll need them. The water's frigid."

By the time they got to the beach, Zoey suddenly felt as happy and free as she'd ever felt in her whole life. The waves rolled up smooth and huge onto the sloping, fine-sand beach. And when Anika's brother handed Zoey the surfboard, she felt as if someone had just put the whole world and all its answers right into her bare hands.

*   *   *

"Okay, now check the bracket size in that brickwork," Guy shouted up to Lucas.

Lucas was poised on a ladder twelve feet above the gallery level of the lighthouse, checking the brackets that attached the top section of the spiral staircase to the walkway surrounding the lantern. Below, Guy's tape player was blasting the frenzied screams of twenty thousand fans from an old Grateful Dead live-in-concert tape.

Lucas looked down over his shoulder. "These are eight-inch brackets," he yelled down.

"I bought six inchers," Guy cried.

"There's an eight incher at the bottom of your toolbox," Lucas replied. "We can start with that. Why don't you pass it up and I'll see if it's a good match?"

Lucas stepped down one rung of the ladder and stretched out his hand. He and Guy had been inspecting and repairing some minor structural problems near the top of the lighthouse all day. After that they planned to reinforce the staircase, replace some of the interior masonry, then work with a master craftsman to clean and renovate the Fresnel lens.

"Where'd you figure out how to reinforce a hundred-forty-year-old steel staircase?" Guy called out, rummaging through the toolbox. He reached over and turned down the music. "I thought fishermen were strictly wood folk."

"Like I told you, my dad got a kick out of making me his unpaid apprentice."

Guy grunted out a laugh. "Convenient."

Lucas nodded as Guy climbed halfway up the ladder and handed him the bracket. Then Lucas climbed back and held the bracket up to the old one.

"What's it look like?"

Lucas glanced down. "That'll do it. The walkway's underside has some rust, but it's pretty solid. I think it will work great."

"Hallelujah," Guy muttered. "New metalwork was all I needed to run over budget with the Lighthouse Preservation Society."

"Okay," Lucas said, twisting out the last ancient bolt with his wrench. He climbed down the ladder and put his hands on his hips. "Now all we need is twenty-three more of the same size, and we're there."

Guy sat down on the top step and pulled out a pouch of tobacco to roll himself a cigarette. "Take a break, Cabral, or I'll have to raise your hourly wage."

Lucas shrugged. He reached for his backpack and took out a thermos of coffee. "Sure."

"So," Guy said. He pinched a wad of tobacco into the rectangle of cigarette paper, then deftly rolled it with both thumbs and forefingers. "Your dad's gone now, huh?"

Lucas looked at him, wondering how Guy could possibly know that as he poured a shallow cup into his plastic thermos cap. "Yep. It was pretty sudden. A heart attack."

Guy gave him a wry smile. "I did some checking up on you," he confessed.

For a moment Lucas was horrified.

"Relax," Guy said. "I know all about your two years in Youth Authority, too, but I heard you're an upstanding kid from a number of reliable sources. So that's good enough for me."

Lucas let out a long breath as Guy sealed his cigarette with a lick, then stuck it between his lips, shaking his head. He drew out a packet of matches from his shirt pocket and lit the tip, inhaling deeply and giving Lucas a sideways glance. "Hey, don't give me that politically correct look of disapproval."

Lucas laughed, gulping his coffee. "I'm not. It's your guilty conscience getting to you."

Guy waved him off. "Yeah, you're right. Either that or my girlfriend. She doesn't like these things."

At the word *girlfriend* Lucas felt his smile fade. He unscrewed his thermos again and poured himself another cup.

"You got a girlfriend, Lucas?"

Lucas looked at him. "I did have a girlfriend, but she broke it off. She's going to Berkeley now."

"Mmmm. Berkeley. Very hip."

"No," Lucas said, almost too quickly. He took a sip of his coffee. "She's not like that."

There was a long silence, which Guy finally broke. "So your dad's gone and your girlfriend's gone. What are you going to do now? Do you want to be a fisherman?"

"No," Lucas said. "I'm just trying to help my mother out until I figure out what else to do."

Guy leaned back against the lighthouse wall and took another long drag of his cigarette. "You can keep on working for me—on weekends or whenever you've got time. Okay?"

Lucas straightened up. "Really?"

Guy shrugged. "Sure. And there are plenty more jobs ahead of me when this lighthouse project is done, if you're interested. I'm sort of a small operation because I like it that way, but I do a lot of restoration work on historic buildings all up and down the New England coast. I have about twenty people working for me right now."

Lucas was surprised. "Then—what are you doing all alone on this project?"

Guy grinned at him. "I'm like you, man. Sometimes I just like to work alone." He swept his hand toward the window. "Get up above it all."

"I'm interested," Lucas said quietly.

"You should be," Guy told him, taking another peaceful puff. "It's a good living."

LUCAS

Dear Zoey,

I don't know if you have
my first letter. Or if you
even read it. But I'm
writing you again on the off
chance that the first one
never arrived. I feel kind
of like I'm sending a
bottle out to sea with a
note rolled up in it.

I'm working my dad's boat
about five days a week
right now, barely snagging
enough to bring in the
grocery and utility money for
my mom. I don't know how he

did it for so long. I really
don't know what they lived
on. On the weekends I've
been working on a restoration
project up at the Blue
Rock Lighthouse. Wish you
could see the work we're
doing and see the view out
the top window of the
islands and the sea beyond.
It's really so beautiful.
   I've had more time to
think, of course. That's the
beauty of spending so much
time alone. It kind of
reminds me of the two years
I spent at Youth Authority,
separated from the things
and the people I loved,

wondering what the hell I was doing and spending a lot of time staring at a picture of you taped to the wall above my bed.

I've decided something. I will not give up on what I feel for you because I know it's the best thing I've ever felt or done in my life. to have loved you.

I've waited for you before, and I will wait again.

As long as it takes, Zoey. I have nothing but time.

Love,

Lucas

Ten

"Nina!" The Buzzard screeched. Nina had just walked into the school office, and the sound of The Buzzard's voice jarred Nina's already fragile nerves almost to the breaking point. She grimaced and lifted the hinged section of the front counter, making her way to the front desk, where The Buzzard was sitting.

"Yes, Mrs. Billington?" Nina asked sweetly, realizing that her sarcasm was wasted on this audience but unable to stop herself, anyway.

"Nina. Please get me a cup of coffee and ask Lionel if he would like one as well." The Buzzard's mouth pursed when she said "Lionel," overemphasizing Principal Higgins' first name, which made Nina wonder briefly whether there was something going on between them. She took another look at The Buzzard, then shook the thought away, repulsed.

"Coffee's not good for you, Mrs. Billington," Nina said evenly. "It can become addictive."

"Thank you, Miss Geiger," The Buzzard

snapped, turning to answer the phone. "I like it with milk."

After taking the principal's order, Nina clomped out to the kitchenette, desperately wishing for a way out of her nerd job in the office. If only she hadn't fallen in love with that cute guy working here—who'd quit almost the next minute—and signed a contract indenturing her to slavery with The Buzzard for the rest of the school year.

Nina briefly considered spitting in the coffee but decided against it. It wouldn't be any fun unless The Buzzard found out about it, anyway.

Finally Nina returned with the coffee. "I place this cup before you with deepest reservations."

The Buzzard glared. "Nina," she said slowly, "there's something I'd like you to do for me."

"I'm sorry, I'm busy right now, Mrs. Billington."

"Don't worry—I'll take the phones. Since I am supposed to rest my hip, I am unable to make the rounds of the freshman homerooms this morning to deliver my annual talk on school safety and emergency fire procedures," The Buzzard said crisply. "I've decided that your speaking voice, while not as voluminous as mine, is passable, and I want you to do it."

Nina stared at her, horrified.

The Buzzard handed her a laminated sheet. "Here is my presentation. I think you will find it clear and concise. Just read it, please, without embellishment. The homeroom teachers are expecting you. Here is the schedule."

Nina couldn't breathe. The Buzzard's annual safety speech was the highlight of everyone's freshman year—students had been parodying it for years. In fact, Nina had been mimicking the famous "Roll *about* to put the flames *out*" section just the week before. "I—I can't," she stammered.

"Why not?"

"I—have stage fright," Nina said earnestly. She could almost see her reputation at Weymouth High disintegrating before her very eyes. She'd sunk to the lowest of the low; she was The Buzzard's pawn.

"Then this will be good for you," The Buzzard said briskly. "And I have one other errand for you. There's still time before your first presentation."

Nina felt faint.

"We received an important shipment this morning that needs to be delivered immediately to the gymnasium," The Buzzard went on in her precise way. She pointed a bony finger into the front office, where two large boxes sat on a cart. "Please take them at once."

Nina sighed. She loathed the gymnasium. But at least there was some two hundred yards of fresh air between the front office and the gym. She decided to make the trip last as long as possible in order to delay her fire safety humiliation.

The halls were eerily empty. Once outside, the cart bumped noisily over the cracked asphalt path to the gym. Nina felt, for some reason, sadder and lonelier than she had ever felt in her life. Everyone who had been important to her was gone. Everyone except Lucas, who was small comfort now, thanks to Lara. Now every move she made with Lucas was something that could be taken the wrong way—even in her own mind.

What I need, she thought, *is some more friends. I need to make more of an effort. Maybe I could be friendly and make conversation.* This didn't seem too likely, but Nina decided she would try it out for a little while and see how it went.

Nina looked up, realizing that she was standing at the doorway to the gym. She wasn't sure what to do with her delivery.

"Yes?" the varsity football coach boomed. "May we help you?"

The entire varsity football team was assembled on the bleachers in front of him, along with every member of the cheerleading squad and drill team. *Are they having their own private pep rally?* she wondered.

"Um," Nina said. "Mrs. Billington said you were waiting for this delivery."

"What's the delivery?" the coach asked, checking his watch impatiently.

Nina looked in one of the boxes and pulled out a blue-and-white pom-pom. "Pom-poms from Portland Sports Image and . . ." Nina looked at the label under plastic on the second cardboard box, which was still taped shut. "Fifty cups."

Several of the cheerleaders tittered.

"The cups are from the same store," Nina went on, oblivious.

"What size?" one deep-voiced football player called out.

Nina looked up in confusion, then looked down again and read the label. "Large," she said. Then, in an effort to be friendly and conversational, she added, "I guess you jocks get pretty thirsty."

There were outright chuckles now. The coach smiled and turned slightly pink. The head cheerleader, Amber Robertson, drew her hands up to her mouth in shock. Soon the entire group was howling with laughter while Nina stood there in her camouflage pants, black T-shirt, and Dr. Marten boots, not understanding why everyone was laughing and wondering whether there was a piece of food stuck to her face.

"Get a grip, Nina," one of the drill team members whispered to her. "They're protective athletic cups for the guys. Don't just stand there like an idiot."

Finally understanding, Nina shoved the cart across the room with the heel of her boot and walked out, wishing that she had told the team that the cups were size minuscule.

She sighed. "Roll *about* to put the flames *out*," she practiced, steeling herself for the further humiliations that were sure to come.

Eleven

First there was the scent of barely scorched cloth. The good smell you got when you ironed a dress in the kitchen on a warm evening just before going out.

Then the merest shift in odor. Not scorched, really. Singed. The edge of a garment, caught briefly in flame and quickly put out.

Lara began to realize that she was free-floating in a void, unable to move or see. The only sensation was of smell and sound, and the smell grew stronger.

Smoke. Bare wisps of it, as if she were walking down a country lane in autumn, smelling the heaps of fall leaves burning in nearby pastures.

Again she struggled to move, but she seemed to have no body to move. The smoke thickened slightly, as if an ember from the burning leaves had caught the grass, and a small flame had begun to lick its way across the field toward her.

She tried to stir, but her mind was disconnected

from anything solid. There were thoughts and a wild, swinging panic, but all was taking place in the midst of a silent darkness and paralysis.

"Lara?" she heard her father ask. "Lara?"

Billowing smoke curled around where her head was supposed to be, creeping into her mouth and nose. She tried to open her mouth to scream but remembered that she had no mouth. She was invisible except for the smoke that filled the paralyzed void within.

The smoke was heavy now, thick as ashes, choking her. Somewhere near she heard her father's calls turn into screams. She prayed for air and light and then realized that she was rushing through space. The air cleared and she could breathe now, though she could still hear the agonized cries somewhere below, until they were silent.

"No!" Lara gasped. She jerked her head up off the pillow and frantically scattered the dream smoke away from her face. She leaped off the bed and sat down hard on the floor to brush the flames from her feet.

"I'm awake," Lara suddenly whispered, stopping and looking around her. The solid ground: a pale green carpet. Walls. Furniture. Her own body, sweating and shivering.

Lara fell over on her side, weeping and staring

into the darkness. Nothing made sense. Sure, she might have expected this kind of night terrors if she'd been drinking a lot. But she had been totally, achingly dry for the past two weeks.

She had no idea why this was happening now—now that she was finally climbing out of the pit that had been her life for so many years. And it wasn't even like she was turning into a Zoey clone, walking around in little ironed blouses or anything.

It was something different. She knew that she was slowly uncovering a part of herself that was good and that didn't have anything to do with Zoey. The only problem now, though, was that the nightmares were threatening to drag her right back down to her old messed-up self.

In fact, at this very moment she had a burning desire to drink the entire contents of the flask she'd hidden under Zoey's bed.

Lara got up off the floor and switched on the lamp next to the bed. She yanked a tissue out of the box, blew her nose, then slipped back in between the sheets, too tired to stay awake and too wired to sleep.

Yesterday, Lara remembered, her dad had played an old Doors recording from the sixties. There was one really bad, slow song he used to play so much that the vinyl was totally scratched. But while they were listening to it, the needle suddenly slipped and caught onto a groove in the next cut, which sang out clear and beautiful.

That's what had happened to her, Lara thought. She'd slipped, almost accidentally, into a cleaner groove. Her anger hadn't gone away, but she was pouring it onto canvas instead of letting it squash her over and over again.

Maybe it was a kind of weird payback for her various misdeeds on Chatham Island, Lara thought miserably, staring up at the dark ceiling. Maybe the gods were looking down and punishing her for telling Zoey the truth about Nina and Lucas, for instance. Maybe they were punishing her for any of a million things she had done.

Lara rose out of bed and shook off her thoughts. The house was quiet except for the low sound of her father snoring in the room across the hall.

She pulled her drawing board and paper out from under the bed, sat them on her knees, then arranged several pastels on the bedside table next to her. The image of a face appeared in her mind, and she bent to the paper. She worked quickly and crazily, shading and coloring the eyes before she even knew the shape of the head. Man or woman? It was just a face full of pain. A face she recognized, although she couldn't put her finger on why or how.

Light gradually rose through the window, and she heard stirring in the master bathroom. Footsteps descended into the downstairs hallway.

She shifted back to the drawing board and looked into eyes she'd drawn, which were staring back at her. The face had flowed out of her like an open channel, so quickly it felt as if her hand were being controlled by something other than her own mind.

"Lara?" She heard Ms. Passmore's voice.

"Yeah?"

"Are you up?"

Lara looked up from her drawing. "Yeah. Come in."

The door opened, and Ms. Passmore stuck her head in. She was wearing a flowered bathrobe, and her faded blond hair was half pulled back.

Ms. Passmore sat down at the foot of the bed and yawned. "What are you doing up so early?"

Lara shrugged. "I don't know."

"Mmmm." Ms. Passmore glanced at the drawing board. "May I see?"

Lara dropped to her knees and turned the drawing around so that it was facing Ms. Passmore. "It's just a face I was playing around with."

Ms. Passmore turned serious. She touched the corner of the paper and pulled it toward her. "Lara," she said softly. "This is—really good."

Lara pulled a tissue out of the box and coughed into it. "Um, thanks."

"I hope you show this one to Sandy," Ms. Passmore said, pausing. "Who is this?"

"I don't know," Lara replied, shaking her head.

Ms. Passmore bit her lip, then patted Lara's leg. "Keep it up, Lara. You're good. Really good." She drew in her breath and let out a deep chuckle. "I can't *believe* how good."

"Thank you," Lara said, joining her laugh. For a moment they just sat there together, smiling, and Lara had a brief longing to spill everything, to tell Ms. Passmore all about the nightmares.

Something must have showed on her face. "What is it?" Ms. Passmore asked.

Lara opened her mouth to speak, then closed it. What if she did talk about her dreams? What if she did collapse into honesty and confess the whole pit of her unconscious, which was now haunting her every time she shut her eyes? How was that supposed to help? What could possibly happen except that they'd suspect her of being deeply unhappy, flipped out, and using drugs again?

Nope, Lara told herself, turning her drawing board around again as Ms. Passmore stepped out of the room. What Lara needed to do now was pull her head down, do her art, and keep her mouth firmly shut.

I've finally reached a place where I can be happy, Lara thought contentedly, flipping her pencil down and continuing with the sketch. She worked the eyes again, turning them from smoky blue to darkness itself. The mouth was drawn down now as if it were twisting in agony. Her fingers moved the pencil along the side of the face, drawing out long wisps of hair, blown back and up. The shape of the mouth again . . .

Lara stopped drawing and pushed the sheet away from her for a moment as if to see it more clearly. She frowned. The face *was* familiar yet wore an expression so foreign to it that Lara had taken a long time to recognize it. She pushed the drawing away, not wanting to look at what she saw there.

The face was Ms. Passmore's.

Claire

Dear Nina,

 I'm just writing to let you
know what you can look forward
to next year, since I'm sure
you're dying of curiosity.

 Living in a dorm is not as
exciting as I thought it'd be.
Maybe it's because most
everyone's a freshman and
we're all sort of trying to figure
out what we're doing. People
seem to either study all the time
or drink beer and listen to Bob
Marley.

This may sound totally bizarre, but sometimes I actually think about all the good times back on the island before we went our separate ways. I sometimes just want to think about all the quiet sounds of the island and how they used to calm me down when things got out of control. Chatham Island is, after all, a really beautiful place, Nina. Do we ever really appreciate what we have until it s gone?

Another thing: Although it is really exciting to live in a big city, it has its flip side. I never realized how reassuring it was to be surrounded by people who'd known me almost my whole life. I know it seems irritating to you now, but wait until nobody knows you! Believe me, that's worse.

Well, I guess I should get back to work. It seems weird not to be able to climb up to my widow's walk and stare out at the sky. It seems weird not to have you around, too. I'm a little worried that you'll have the upper hand when I get home; I'll be so out of practice with the put-downs.

Believe it or not, I miss you

a lot. I haven't met anyone here
with your sense of humor.
   Take care!
                    Love,
                    Claire

Twelve

"I bought you something," Claire told Jake on Tuesday night before they turned out the light to sleep.

"Oh, man." Jake groaned, turning over. He thought with relief of the room he might have snagged in one of BU's older dorms. If everything worked as planned, he'd have it in just a few days, taking the place of a student who'd broken his leg and suddenly needed a ground-floor room. "What did you get me?"

"Something in chiffon."

"Come on, Claire. Have mercy."

There was a contented sigh in the bed across the dark room. "I *did* have mercy on you, remember? Besides, this is fun. And we haven't gotten caught yet, have we?"

"No," Jake hedged.

"Anyway," Claire went on. "I went back to my favorite thrift shop and found a pretty white chiffon robe. Size sixteen."

"I'm a woman's fourteen."

"In the hips, but not the shoulders," Claire reminded him. "Please continue with the slippers, and if you wish, you may replace the shower cap with a towel over the head," she went on.

"Thanks, Claire," Jake said glumly. "I've been hoping to change my look."

"I bought you a nice wig and a sporty lavender sweatshirt for the day after tomorrow."

"Wonderful."

"I thought it would be a nice change," Claire said charitably.

"Thank you, Claire. Good night."

"Good night."

"More mail from Maine," Anika announced, dropping three letters, a postcard, and a hand-addressed parcel on Zoey's desk. "I get irritating phone calls and E-mail messages. You get actual letters and packages."

Zoey smiled at a letter with her mother's handwriting on it. "My parents are a throwback to a kinder, gentler age. They write letters all the time and read books other than those recommended by Oprah Winfrey."

Anika sat down at her computer and flicked it on. "I bet they don't even wear pagers."

"Nope," Zoey said absently, setting her mom's letter on her desk, then staring at the next one, which had Lucas's familiar scrawl on it. Beneath it was an envelope with Nina's crazy lettering. She looked away, out the window at the afternoon light on the Berkeley Hills.

Zoey crossed the room and threw Nina and Lucas's unopened letters in the wastepaper basket.

Anika looked up, startled. "What's up?"

Zoey turned to face her. "Junk mail," she said.

Anika nodded, although she looked dubious. "Are you still coming with us for Moroccan food?" she wanted to know.

Zoey checked her watch. "Yeah. I asked Kevin—remember him from the other day?—if he wanted to come along. It's a big group, anyway, isn't it?"

"Yep," Anika said. "A bunch of my friends from San Rafael. Two are at Stanford, three are at Santa Cruz, and one is bumming around with a ridiculously huge trust fund. Remind me to make her pay."

"Sure," Zoey said, grabbing her shower things.

"We're meeting them there in forty-five minutes," Anika yelled.

"Kevin's going to wait in the lobby for us," Zoey called out.

She hurried down the hall and quickly showered, blew her long blond hair slightly dry, then dabbed her lips with gloss. Ten minutes later she was wearing clean jeans, a white T-shirt, and a used man's vest she'd bought for a dollar two days before at a Berkeley flea market.

"Let's grab Kevin and go," Anika said, still wearing a big worn sweater over black leggings and no makeup. Large dangly silver earrings shook against her cheeks. "I'm starved."

"Kevin asked me out, actually," Zoey confessed in the elevator. "I like him, but I didn't want to get into a date thing. So I invited him to this."

Anika shrugged. "Whatever works. You might end up changing your mind, though."

Zoey found herself staring up at the elevator ceiling and suddenly picturing Lucas's face. His brown eyes. The smile that made his whole face crinkle up . . .

"Hi!" A guy's voice broke her thoughts.

The elevator door had opened and there stood Kevin, looking sheepish in jeans and a new-looking shirt. Zoey had to blink and adjust her thoughts. Kevin was no Lucas, of course. But he was okay, Zoey told herself. He was an okay friend.

"Come on, Kevin," Anika said, instantly slipping her arm around Kevin's elbow and dragging him toward the door to the parking garage. "This is going to be an interesting night. My friend Eva says she's got a surprise for us."

Zoey tilted back her head and laughed at Anika's ice-breaking techniques, trotting behind them while Kevin shouted in mock protest.

A few minutes later Anika had pulled the van into a dingy parking lot behind a row of shops and restaurants on College Avenue. "The Marakesh Express is in front," Anika explained, slamming the van door. "Look for the bright green door with the palm trees painted on it."

Zoey giggled and was still laughing when they crowded into the jam-packed restaurant— a dark, low-ceilinged place hung with exotic fabrics. Lively Moroccan music filled the room, and when she began looking at the tables, she saw that they were very low and surrounded by pillows, where people were sitting and eating. She stared and nudged Kevin in the ribs. "We're eating on the floor," she said, surprised and somewhat delighted.

Kevin nodded. "I know. You sort of lounge around on pillows and eat with your hands."

"Anika! Over here!" someone called, and Zoey turned. "We've already ordered."

Anika waved and trooped across the

crowded room, greeting her friends and giving each one a joyful hug.

Zoey sat down cheerfully next to Kevin on the other side of the table from Anika, who was already telling stories and pretending to recite poetry. A dark man in white poured warm water into a bowl next to her plate out of a huge silver teapot, then draped her lap with a white cloth. She peeked over at Kevin, who was washing his hands seriously and wiping them with the cloth.

"If my friends could see me now," Zoey said, and laughed.

Kevin smiled. "What do you mean? What would they say?"

Zoey opened her mouth to reply, then, thinking better of it, ate something instead. "Delicious!" she exclaimed.

"Figs!" Anika called out from across the table. "You've got to try the fresh figs, Zoey. Hey, everyone. This is Zoey Passmore, my roommate from the beautiful state of Maine who actually lives on an island."

Zoey glanced around the table and smiled at everyone. There was a thin guy with tiny spectacles and a beard, a tanned girl with piercing blue eyes and straw-colored hair worn in intricate cornrows, two friendly-looking women in sweaters, and a jovial-looking African-American guy with a face that was almost perfectly round.

"And this is Kevin," Anika said exuberantly, "who sits next to Zoey in Twentieth-Century lit!" Anika pointed around the table. "These are my best friends, Roger, Eva, Karen, Anne, and Larry."

Zoey waved and ate a fig. Then she ate something that was rice with leaves wrapped around it. Then lamb ribs. Then something very sweet and crunchy with honey and mint. She found herself giving in to the rhythm of the music and Anika's stories, which were easily matched by her friends.

After an hour Anika's blond friend, Eva, looked at her watch and stood up on her knees. "It's time to go, everyone."

Everyone at the table groaned. A live Moroccan band had taken over, and the place was rocking.

"Wait!" Anika called out. "Eva said she had some kind of surprise. What is it? Spit it out."

Eva's pretty face got very serious and secretive. Slowly, and with great drama, she dug her hand into her purse, then swiftly pulled out a handful of tickets, which she waved in the air.

Anika immediately grabbed one and let out a joyful cry. "Counting Crows!" She looked at the ticket again, gasped, and clutched it to her breast. "And it starts in one hour at Memorial Stadium."

Zoey was stunned.

"Whoa!" Kevin yelled.

"As soon as I heard it on the radio I speed-dialed Ticketmaster and bought ten tickets," Eva confessed. Then she laughed. "I already scalped the rest."

Zoey jumped up from the table with the others and dug a twenty-dollar bill out of her back pocket, which she slipped to Eva, the trust fund baby who was signing a credit card slip. "Let me. Please."

Eva waved the money away. "Forget it. It's cool."

Only a few minutes later Zoey, Kevin, and Anika were zooming back up to the campus and parking the van in the stadium lot, already milling with fans.

Linking arms with Kevin and Anika, Zoey skipped toward the huge stadium until they were funneled with thousands of other students and fans into the main ramp leading inside.

"My parents always come here for the big game with Stanford." Anika laughed. "Big Cal Berkeley fans and all. But this is totally better than a football game."

"Check it out," Kevin cried as they worked their way toward their seats. Below, the stage was set up on the field, brightly lit and jammed with equipment. But what struck Zoey most was the view that stretched out straight ahead of them.

The sky was a deep powder blue, turning vanilla toward the horizon, which hit just past the shining white city of San Francisco across the bay. To the right was the spidery red Golden Gate Bridge and farther over, the fluffy white of the late summer fog pouring over the Sausalito hills.

To the left a slow moon was rising in the sky, and Zoey stared at it, temporarily oblivious to the roar of the crowd and the stirring of the opening act below on the stage.

It was the same moon, of course, that she'd stared at a hundred thousand times before on Chatham Island. And yet it really was a different moon hovering over an entirely different world—more immediate and full of energy than she'd ever imagined her world could be.

"Kevin," Zoey said spontaneously, turning to share her thought with Kevin, who was sitting next to her.

Kevin was laughing at something one of Anika's friends had said. Then he turned, still laughing, to Zoey. "What?"

"I—I . . . ," Zoey stammered, looking into his laughing brown eyes, searching for something—she wasn't sure what. But whatever she was looking for, it wasn't there. "Nothing," she said.

Zoey smiled and looked away.

She forced herself to drain her mind of all her troubles. Instead she focused only on the music—sad songs that belonged to someone else.

Thirteen

Benjamin closed his eyes and tried to sleep. He'd caught a 6:30 A.M. train from Penn Station, hoping to rest on the way to his Thursday-morning appointment with Dr. Martin in Boston. But the fretful sway of the train was making it impossible.

He opened his eyes and stared out the window, barely able to see the crumbling backsides of the inner-city buildings sliding by. His mood, already dark, grew worse, and he shut his eyes again.

Benjamin sighed. This was one of his problems. He knew he needed to rest his eyes to save them, yet the darkness was the very thing that made him afraid. He'd lived for the day when he could see, yet now that he could, it seemed as if all he did was live in fear of recurring blindness. In fact, Benjamin admitted to himself, he was terrified.

He shook his head, remembering what Helen Keller had once said about security.

Actually, Benjamin remembered bitterly, she'd said that there's really no such thing. Helen Keller believed that it didn't really matter whether a person tried to avoid danger and pain or whether he attacked his life head-on like a fearless crazy man.

The fearful are caught as often as the bold.

Benjamin opened his eyes and stared at the grubby seat back in front of him. He used to think Helen Keller was talking about freedom. But now he decided she was saying something much darker. Helen Keller was saying that it didn't matter what you did. You were controlled by fate, anyway.

By the time he reached Boston, his back was damp with sweat and his head was throbbing. It was another fifteen minutes on a bus down Massachusetts Avenue before he walked into Dr. Martin's reception room.

"Hi, Benjamin," the middle-aged receptionist said cheerfully.

Benjamin smiled at her weakly and sat down on the couch facing a fan of *People* magazines on the coffee table. On the walls were color underwater photographs of exotic fish and another photograph of Dr. Martin standing on a tropical beach in scuba diving gear.

A minute later a door opened and Dr. Martin stepped out. He wore a white jacket and brilliant silk tie that set off his dark, coffee-colored skin.

"Good to see you, Benjamin," Dr. Martin said, shaking his hand and looking curiously into his eyes.

"Glad I can see you, too, Dr. Martin," Benjamin said, following him down the hallway he'd once memorized in darkness. "What did you do? Take my surgery fees and haul down to the Caribbean?"

"I needed a vacation," Dr. Martin said dryly, pointing to the examination chair and pulling a large piece of machinery out of a corner. "Belize. I went scuba diving."

"You're too used to my harassment," Benjamin complained. "It's no fun anymore."

"Nope," Dr. Martin said absently, looking at a chart while his assistant put dilation drops in Benjamin's eyes. A few minutes later he was sitting up, his chin affixed to the plastic pad in the center of Dr. Martin's complex machinery.

"Okay, watch the red light, please, Benjamin," Dr. Martin said quietly.

Benjamin stared patiently into the beam of light.

"So you're at Columbia now?" Dr. Martin said, sitting absolutely still as he clicked something in the machine.

"Yeah."

"And how's it going?

"This has me a little distracted."

"Mmmm," Dr. Martin said. "Uh-huh. Mmmmm."

Benjamin didn't like those sounds. In fact, he wasn't liking anything about this trip to Boston.

"Okay. You can sit back now." Dr. Martin rolled his stool back, crossed his arms, and looked up at the ceiling.

Benjamin felt sick.

"You've had a setback," Dr. Martin said.

Benjamin looked at him. "How bad is it?"

"You've had another partial retinal detachment in your left eye," Dr. Martin said calmly. "It's a common reaction when the eye has not had sufficient rest following surgery."

Benjamin closed his eyes in frustration.

"That was why I prescribed rest for you last winter," Dr. Martin continued. "Jarring of the eyes, especially in their delicate, postoperative condition, commonly makes things worse."

"Yeah, but I had more fun than I'd had in seven years."

"Benjamin," Dr. Martin said seriously. "It was only natural for you to cut loose a little after you had your sight back. From what your parents have told me, you were doing a lot of surfing, photography, reading, and spending time in the sun. . . ."

"Of course I did," Benjamin snapped. "Wouldn't you have?"

Dr. Martin sighed. "Your surgery was for severe macular degeneration, Benjamin. The healing process of the delicate blood vessels in your retina cannot take place if you are involved in high-impact sports."

"Sorry."

"Don't apologize to me. Think about your life. I'll be plain. You have to slow it down, or you could lose your sight again."

Benjamin realized that his entire body had gone numb. "What do you want me to do?"

"We're going to have to repair your detached retina in the left eye, for starters," Dr. Martin said quietly.

"Oh, man," Benjamin moaned.

"Then I'm going to recommend a new laser treatment called photocoagulation."

"What?"

"You're beginning to develop some abnormal and extremely fragile blood vessels in the choroid underlying the retina of both eyes. When they break, as they are beginning to, your sight begins to fail."

"The lasers seal them off?" Benjamin asked.

"Exactly. In the past the therapy has been helpful with patients just beginning to experience the problem, but we've got a new experimental photocoagulation treatment at Boston

General for advanced cases like yours. I'd like to see if it could help you."

Benjamin shook his head. "Come on. There's got to be something in New York like that. Right?"

"Wrong. Boston General has the first of its kind. It's a treatment that takes about an hour, once a week for ten weeks."

"Well, I live in New York now. How am I going to manage that?"

Dr. Martin laid one hand heavily on Benjamin's shoulder as he headed toward the door. "You try to work things out, Benjamin. Then let me know what you've decided. But don't take any chances. You don't want to go through life in darkness again."

Aisha

Do you know what's weird?
Not knowing anyone.

In North Harbor, I always
knew what to think of someone
before I had even spoken to
them. Because even if you
don't know someone, you know
all about them.

But here I don't know
anything about anyone, except
where they go to college.
Anyone who chose to lie to me
or misrepresent themselves
would find me an easy victim,
I guess.

Like my roommate, for
example. She seems nice, but

every now and again she'll do
something that I don't know
how to interpret. Like she'll
make plans to meet me at the
dining center for lunch, then
stand me up. Back home I
would know whether she was
malicious or just a space cadet.

Only a few years on Chatham
Island has effectively
destroyed my memory of how
to get to know people. I guess
you just give them the benefit
of the doubt for a while.

Right?

Fourteen

Claire had been lying awake in her dorm bed since 3 A.M. Her head hurt from reading until midnight, but the thought of getting up and walking down the hall to take two aspirin exhausted her.

She stared up at the ceiling, stung by a sudden and inexplicable homesickness. She found herself pretending that the little white bumps on its cottage cheese surface were really stars stretched across the dark sky, but the wail of a passing police car destroyed the mood.

Claire shut her eyes tightly and turned over in the bed. Maybe it was just her restlessness and the fact that back home, she usually went up to the widow's walk at the top of her house when she had trouble sleeping. *That was one thing about Chatham Island*, Claire thought, *there were plenty of broad views, meandering trails, and empty beaches to ponder.* She'd never realized how these things made it easier to really think.

Her skin felt hot. She kept seeing the image of her sister, Nina's, face. Her father's. She had a sudden longing to go downstairs into her home's big kitchen and fix herself a snack from their perpetually well-stocked fridge.

She realized that her throat was tight with inexpressible feelings. She was going to have to get over this. After all, she'd started a new life. She couldn't go back now.

And yet something made her begin counting the days until the October break.

"Letter for you, Nina!" Mrs. Geiger was calling from the kitchen as Nina arrived home from school.

Nina rolled her eyes as she pushed open the kitchen door. Her stepmother and Janelle hovered over the massive cooking island, where a giant rack of meat glistened on a copper roasting pan.

"What's going on?" Nina drawled. "Are Fred and Wilma Flintstone coming for dinner?"

Mrs. Geiger smiled patiently. "This is a rack of lamb, Nina. It's your father's favorite dish."

"It is also the favorite dish of the lumbering jackal," Nina said with drama, dropping her book bag and heading for the fridge. "I saw it on the Discovery Channel."

"We got you your favorite chicken salad

from the Weymouth Deli this morning," Janelle said, trimming the last bit of fat from the bones and standing back to admire the roast.

"It's lovely," Mrs. Geiger said. "We'll just surround it with the baby potatoes and stick it in at three-fifty." She turned to Nina. "There's a letter for you next to the phone."

For a dizzy moment Nina was positive the letter was from Zoey. *Oh, thank God,* she thought. *Thank God, she wrote back.* Then fear seized her heart. What would Zoey's letter say? What if it said that she never wanted to be friends again? Nina nearly ran to the phone, frantic.

"It's from Claire!" she nearly shouted, a thousand different emotions washing over her at once.

"Terrific!" Mrs. Geiger said. "Dinner's at eight!" she called out mildly as Nina backed through the door, staring at her name and address written in what was definitely Claire's spidery handwriting.

Nina walked slowly upstairs, opened her bedroom door, and flopped on her unmade bed, littered with discarded blouses, socks, granola bar wrappers, and CD covers.

The letter began without fanfare.

Dear Nina,
   I'm just writing to let you know what

*you can look forward to next year, since
I'm sure you're dying of curiosity.*

"What is she driving at?" Nina muttered to herself. She flipped off the lid to the plastic container
with one hand and dug out a forkful of chicken
salad. Then, with it poised in midair, she scanned
down the page. Her mouth began to drop open.

*. . . Island is, after all, a really beauti-
ful place, Nina. Do we ever really appreciate what we have until it's gone?*

Nina looked up at her Pearl Jam poster
sheep. "Claire's gone mad."

*Believe it or not, I miss you a lot. I
haven't met anyone here with your sense
of humor.*

"She needs help," Nina whispered to herself.
"Claire? Have the MIT nerds already given you
a freshman brain tissue transplant?"

*Love,
Claire.*

Love? Nina thought, finally taking her first
huge bite of chicken salad. *You harass and*

168

ignore me for seventeen years, then want to talk about love? You're having delusions, Claire. Student orientation turned your mind inside out. The cafeteria food is tainted with untested herbal sedatives. Piped messages are being delivered to your subconscious while you sleep in your dorm room. Come home, Claire. We're your only hope.

Fifteen

A cold rain began to fall as Lucas swung the last lobster trap up on deck. A swell suddenly rocked the boat, and he felt the cage bash his thumb.

"Son of a . . . ," Lucas sputtered, heaving the trap onto the boat, dropping it, then putting his frozen, jammed finger into his mouth.

For a moment he just stood there, watching the blue-gray morning light rise between the cracks in the clouds. Then he reached down and unhooked the cage. But the trap, like three others that morning, was empty.

Lucas shoved it back into the water and watched as it made a frigid splash, then slowly sank. He headed back to the helm and turned the ignition, planning to head back to North Harbor. Three lobsters were barely enough to pay for gas to Weymouth and back. The only place these guys were going was to his mom's kitchen.

He turned on the ignition and heard the engine struggle to turn over once, slow and grinding, then turned the key backward. He remembered his dad cursing the ignition system at dinner one night a couple of days before his heart attack.

Now, as the swells worsened and the rain thickened, Lucas found himself wanting to kill his dad for doing such a lousy job of keeping up his boat.

But his dad was already dead.

He tried the ignition again, and the engine again failed to catch. Pulling his hood up against the wet and grabbing a flashlight, Lucas threw back the hatch and lowered himself down into the swaying boat hull. Lucas knew it could be a clogged carburetor, or a bad fuel pump, or a gunked-up fuel filter. Whatever it was, it was going to keep him stranded in the middle of the channel unless he figured out a way to get it started.

Lucas pointed his flashlight into the greasy mess and checked the jets on the carburetor, which were clogged with grease. Bracing himself against the ever-increasing swells, he pulled his pocketknife out of his back pocket, yanked it open with his teeth, and pulled out the metal toothpick. Then with painstaking effort he cleaned and picked away at the jets until they were clear.

Half an hour later, drenched and freezing, Lucas finally turned the engine over, pulled anchor, and headed home.

"Where have you been?" his mother asked when he finally arrived home. She was small and fair, with thickening ankles and deep circles under her eyes. As always she was in the kitchen, this morning bent over a floured board, kneading pastry dough.

Lucas tore his boots off in the mud room, then yanked down the shoulder straps of his rubber overalls. He paused to calm himself, then hung them slowly on the wall peg.

"I had some trouble with the boat, Mom," Lucas called out, turning on the faucet over the big washtub and dunking his head under it. A clean towel waited for him on the shelf, just as it had for his father a thousand times before.

"What's wrong?" his mother asked, wiping her hands on her apron and walking over to the door.

"The carburetor," Lucas said, scrubbing his hands. "It's in terrible shape. In fact, everything in that boat is about to croak. The engine's . . ."

Lucas looked up and saw that his mother had set her mouth in a line. That straight, tight-jawed line she used to make for his father when he yelled at her.

"Forget it," Lucas said, walking past her through the doorway into the small kitchen, where a place was set for him at the table.

"Your father," his mom reminded him,

"worked hard to keep that boat running, Lucas." She turned away, slipped an oven mitt on her hand, and opened the stove.

"Yeah. Okay." Lucas tipped back his chair and stared at the ceiling.

"Oh, don't give me that," Mrs. Cabral snapped, setting a plate of eggs and ham in front of him. "It's a fine boat, and your father was proud of it."

"The engine needs a complete overhaul, and the hull has some major rot damage, Mom," Lucas said calmly as his mother poured coffee into the cup in front of him. "If we decide to keep it running, we'll have to invest thousands of dollars in the thing."

Mrs. Cabral set the coffeepot down hard. "*If* you keep it running? What do you mean *if*, Lucas?"

"What I mean, Mom," Lucas said carefully, "is that we need to take a hard look at where the money is going to come from now that Dad is gone."

Mrs. Cabral sat down slowly. She stared at her hands, which were twisting the bottom of the apron in her lap. Tears began to fill her eyes. "You never respected what your father did, did you, Lucas?"

"Mom. Dad loved what he did, and I guess I respected him for that. But it's not for me."

Mrs. Cabral looked out the window.

Lucas cleared his throat. "Mom. Let's think about this. We've got an appointment at Social Security tomorrow in Weymouth, and they'll give us a ballpark estimate of what your income from that will be."

She stood up slowly and picked up the rolling pin next to her dough. With quick hands she rolled out a long rectangle, turned it, floured it, then took her pastry knife and sliced it into four sections. "The Passmores say they will hire me to make all the breads and pastries for their restaurant. And with you fishing . . ."

"I don't want to fish, Mom . . . ," Lucas heard himself say.

"It was a good living for your father," Mrs. Cabral replied, shooting him a look and jamming the heel of her hand into one of the dough squares.

"It looks like the lighthouse work I'm doing will get steadier if I want it to, Mom. The income is better and much more reliable than fishing ever was. . . ."

"You never respected your father!" Mrs. Cabral cried.

"I'm not him!" Lucas yelled back, standing up and shoving his chair back. "I'm someone else!"

As they stood there staring at each other,

Lucas remembered how his father used to shout at his mother. And Lucas wondered how true what he had just said really was.

Claire's eyes were still closed, and she had the sensation of being at home in her large bed, with a view to the north of the ocean.

But there was a hollow, metallic knocking sound that clashed with her thoughts. She opened her eyes and sat up in bed. She was in her dorm room in Barron Hall.

Someone was knocking at the door.

Claire's eyes were barely open as she stood up and stumbled to the door. In the dim light she couldn't tell if it was morning or night, but the sound of the insistent knocking was making her so furious, she didn't know what to do except make it stop.

"Yes?" Claire burst out, yanking open the door.

"Hi, Claire."

Claire froze. It was her resident adviser, Julie Sontay, standing there in her bathrobe, looking solemn behind her round glasses.

"Sorry," Julie said, her eyes shifting past Claire's shoulder. "I'm going to have to check your room. There's a story floating around that you're housing a boyfriend."

"What?" Claire drew herself up.

"It's strictly against dorm regs," Julie said

seriously. "The powers that be are coming down hard on this issue, and it's my job to check it out."

"Go away," Claire said firmly, checking her watch. "It's two-thirty in the morning."

But Claire was too late. Julie had pushed open the door with her toe. The doorknob banged against the wall, and all Claire could do was stand there helplessly as Julie stared inside. Claire closed her eyes.

"Okay, Claire," Julie said. "Looks fine to me."

Claire opened her eyes and saw . . . nothing. No Jake. There weren't even sheets on his bed. She let out a relieved sigh, then decided that relief was the wrong emotion to be showing right now. Righteous anger was more like it.

"Of course it looks fine!" Claire huffed. "Now, if you don't mind, I'd like to go back to sleep. And you can tell whoever is spreading that story that I'm hiding my boyfriend in this room to keep her mouth shut! I don't want gossip being spread about me behind my back."

"Of course." Julie looked so sheepish that Claire almost felt sorry for her. After all, Claire had been hiding someone in her room. Just not a boyfriend.

"Good night," Claire said, opening the door so that Julie could leave.

"Good night," Julie replied. "And I'm sorry for the intrusion."

Claire closed the door with a bang. She turned around. "You can come out now, Jake."

The closet door groaned open and a groggy Jake stepped out, his balled-up bed linens in his hand. "I'm impressed that you thought to grab the sheets off the bed," Claire said with a wry smile.

"Quick thinking is always useful around you, Claire."

Claire chuckled. "Sleep tight, Brainiac."

She flipped off the lights.

"Right back at you," Jake said, and soon the gentle sound of his breathing had lulled Claire back into a deep, restful sleep.

When you start word-processing software by double clicking its icon, an empty document window temporarily named Untitled I opens in a window on the screen. If you're ready to begin a new document, you can start typing.

"Okay, okay," Nina muttered to herself, staring as the gray screen flicked open. "I'll start typing."

Nina stared out her bedroom window. Her dad had bought her a Macintosh Performa for

Christmas last year, but it had remained in a box until Benjamin had set it up for her a couple of weeks ago.

The empty screen stared back at her. "So . . . *write*," Nina whispered to herself, leaning back and biting her thumbnail. She reached down for her purse, pulled out a cold Lucky Strike, and stuck it between her lips, where it dangled, unlit.

So far she'd written only one letter to Zoey. Every time she tried, her pen was like a lead weight in her hand. She could barely move it. That's, of course, where she came up with the idea of using her computer. But actually, she thought, she was a really lousy typist. It was probably a bad idea.

Nina heard her father downstairs on the phone. There was the long, low horn of a freighter out at sea. The tapping sound of branches against the house. Every mournful sound reminded her of Zoey.

Nina began writing.

I've been doing a lot of thinking about friendship, Zoey, since I'm sort of living without any right now. It's funny when you think about it. What was it— this thing we had together for so many years?

Nina sat back and stared at her words.

I mean, nothing much really happened. We didn't hitchhike through Europe or win the lottery or set up our own Web page. We went to school. We took the ferry. We talked about love and food and who we saw at the mall. We laughed about stuff.

I guess what I'm trying to say is that we had a sort of conversation that never seemed to end but was totally fascinating to me. I always wanted to know what you thought and how you felt and what your take was on what David Letterman said the night before. That was enough for me.

Zoey: You could have called me up on a brilliant, sunny day in July and said, "Hey, let's lie around inside and read magazines together this afternoon," and you know what? I wouldn't have been able to think of anything else I'd rather do.

Nina lifted her fingers from the keyboard and paused, her eyes filled with tears.

Yes, I've seen Lucas a couple of times, but all he wants to do is talk about you,

Zoey. All he wants is to wrap his head around some way to get you back. To make you understand. Between us it's pretty awkward and painful, to tell you the truth. I don't want Lucas, Zoey—I want my best friend back.

At this point Nina could barely see her computer screen. She lifted her hands to her eyes and wiped away her tears, feeling the salty wet slipping between her fingers. Her chest rose and fell uncontrollably with sobs. After a few minutes, drained, she put her hands back on the keyboard and finished.

And he wants you back, more than maybe you know.
Please write.

>   *Love,*
>   *Nina*

Sixteen

"Two seafood ravioli," Lara called out, pushing through the swinging doors into Passmores' Restaurant's cramped kitchen. She glanced down at the order again. "One chicken piccata. One grilled cod with fennel."

Mr. Passmore took two big plates off the rack next to the gas range and arranged a circle of hot fettucini noodles on each. Then he carefully spooned a sauté of scallops and mushrooms into the center.

Lara pulled open the refrigerator and took out two cold salad plates. She set them down in front of the lettuce bin, then looked at her father over her shoulder. "Is that table four?"

Mr. Passmore glanced at the handwritten slip next to the plates. "Yep. Table four. Two scallop."

Lara thought back. Table four. Window. Redheaded woman with bearded man. "Table four wanted one scallop and one bouillabaisse."

"I need two vegetarian specials," Ms.

Passmore said briskly, passing between the two of them.

Mr. Passmore looked back at Lara and held up her order. "It says two scallop, Lara."

Lara blinked as she arranged the salads. Her eyes were so tired and scratchy, she could barely see. "I blew it, then. Sorry."

"No problem," Mr. Passmore said, sliding the second scallop dish onto the warming table. He wiped his hands down on his apron and checked a pot on the range. "The bouillabaisse is ready, and the scallops are now officially my dinner."

Biting her lower lip, Lara spooned dressing on her salads, slipped past her father's back, and hurried back onto the floor. She cringed. Her father had barely turned his head as she passed him, but his subtle motion wasn't lost on her. She knew he was wondering if she was secretly sucking on vodka between orders. Actually there was a convenient spot just behind the utility closet door. She'd used it before; it could be done.

And why shouldn't he wonder? Lara thought bitterly as she smiled over the table four salads. It was his restaurant. And it wasn't like she'd never turned up at work drunk or completely wasted. The way the kitchen had looked after she accidentally set it on fire was probably still an intensely vivid picture in his mind.

The fire, Lara thought irritably. That didn't especially help her mood. Why did she have to remember that now?

Lara served the salads, greeted three new customers at the door with menus, and filled four water glasses.

"I think you've got this waitressing gig nailed," Ms. Passmore whispered as she sailed by her on her way to the kitchen.

Lara made a face once Ms. Passmore had passed. She knew Ms. Passmore was just trying to keep her spirits up. Maybe it was a mistake to be suspicious of these guys. It was pretty clear that they were willing to forgive her for a whole truckload of things—and not just the mixed-up order.

Still, Lara had to remind herself, she really *wasn't* drinking. She hadn't even had a beer. Or even the merest sip from the trusty flask she had hidden under Zoey's mattress. And all this without a trip to Jake's humiliating A.A. group in Weymouth.

Lara yawned, trudging back to the kitchen to make up a ticket for table one. She was exhausted. When she wasn't working the lunch and dinner shifts at Passmores', she was putting together her drawings for Sandy Krukmeyer. That by itself would have made her incredibly tired. But there were the nightmares, too.

"Jeff said Sandy was stopping by tonight, Lara," Ms. Passmore said, pulling a pan of dinner rolls out of the warming oven.

Lara nodded. "She called this afternoon and said she wanted to look at my new stuff."

"She's got an eight o'clock reservation," Mr. Passmore called out, poking a chicken breast and flipping it over.

"Really?" Lara murmured, doing the math on table one's ticket and trying to sound casual. She'd worked like crazy the night before, but now she was basically terrified to show the drawings she'd done to anyone, especially a big gallery owner. Lara had hidden the one she'd done of Ms. Passmore.

By a quarter to eight Lara had served twelve tables, thirty-five meals, and collected a large wad of bills amounting to sixty-five bucks, which she had hastily counted in the kitchen. She was beginning to catch her breath when a large bird-watching club from Portland entered, having just missed the 7:40 for Weymouth.

"Help me move these tables together, Christopher," Lara said under her breath, leaning up against the bar.

"Whew." Christopher whistled. "It's cha-cha time."

Lara nodded. Her lids were drooping and her feet were aching, but she had an unfamiliar urge to keep going without the screwups. In the midst of taking seventeen separate orders she glimpsed Sandy Krukmeyer entering the restaurant out of the corner of her eye, but there wasn't any time or energy to get nervous.

"Lara," Ms. Passmore said into her ear halfway through the salad course. "Did you bring your portfolio? Sandy wants to take a look at it."

Lara blew her sweaty bangs up, set six bread baskets on her tray, and nodded toward the pantry. "It's on the top shelf, left-hand side, on top of that box of tomato sauce cans."

"I'll take it to her."

There was a big fuss among the bird-watchers over the size of the last two lobsters. Then a spilled scotch and soda, which required Lara to mop up a quarter of the table and replace a soggy side dish of pasta with alfredo sauce. One woman required two aspirin for her head. A small child begged for a chocolate sundae, which Lara made after finding a small can of Hershey's syrup behind several jars of applesauce.

An hour and a half and another twenty-three dollars and fifty cents later, Lara stuck the last dish in the sink and sank down on the stool under the phone.

"I think we made half the mortgage payment tonight," Mr. Passmore said, scraping the grill down with a metal spatula.

Lara stared at the blue flames licking the bottom of the teapot next to the grill, then quickly looked away.

"Lara?"

Lara turned and saw Sandy Krukmeyer at the swinging kitchen door, waving at Mr. Passmore.

"Great crab cakes, Jeff," Sandy called out. She put her hand on Lara's shoulder as Mr. Passmore gave her the peace sign. "Have time to talk?"

Lara's throat suddenly felt dry. "Um. Sure."

They sat down at Sandy's table, next to the window, where a small candle burned in the sill. One of Lara's latest pastel portraits was lying at the top of her portfolio.

"This is wonderful, Lara," Sandy was saying. She slipped on her glasses and stared at it.

Lara glanced nervously at the candle and blew it out.

"You've been working hard," Sandy said. She held up Lara's pastel drawing of a woman's face. It was an ordinary face. A face Lara had seen a thousand times around the docks, hanging over the bar at Passmores', or buying groceries at the marina. But there was a darkness and pain in the eyes that Lara found at once familiar and frightening.

"Look at her eyes," Sandy said softly.

Lara stared at the picture.

"I want to feature your work in my gallery, starting the week before Harvest Festival, Lara," Sandy said all of a sudden. "I'd like to take ten of these right away and have them framed."

"You would?"

"I think you're a major new talent, Lara. And I'm proud to have discovered you."

Seventeen

"Hi, Claire," Jake said softly, cautiously sticking his head into her dorm room.

"Hi," Claire replied, not looking up from her textbook. She was in her nightshirt with a towel on her head.

Jake flopped down onto the spare bed. Claire glanced up, and they looked at each other for a minute. "I didn't get that room I wanted at BU," Jake admitted. "The kid only sprained his ankle. He's going to be fine," he said morosely.

"It's okay," Claire replied evenly. "You can stay here a while longer." She seemed to think for a minute. "And I won't even make you dress like a woman anymore."

"You won't?" Jake asked. Then he seemed to grow suspicious. "Why not?"

Claire smiled. "I called my dad today, and he called the dean. He insisted that I had just had a difficult time on the island and demanded that my RA stop harassing me immediately."

Jake shook his head. "You," he said, "are amazing."

"And don't you forget it," Claire replied. "I'm going to bed," she went on. "Are you ready?"

"Give me five minutes," he said, and snuck down the hall to the rest room.

Claire rubbed lotion into her hands and set her alarm. Jake returned, got under his covers, and seemed to drift off as Claire got into bed and clicked off her lamp. There was the sound of a passing siren outside the window and the steady thump of a stereo in the room next door.

"Claire?" Jake said softly through the darkness.

"Yes?"

"Are you going to miss dressing me up?"

"Shut up, Jake."

There was another long pause before Jake spoke again. "Look—I'm sorry about everything. I really am."

Claire sighed and turned over. "Don't worry about it, Jake. It's kind of nice having you around."

"Good night."

"Good night," Claire said, yawning. A moment later she had begun to float off to sleep when a loud knocking on her door made her sit up straight in bed.

Claire set her jaw. The same loud, relentless

knocking. How could she? Did the MIT housing gestapo actually think this was a legitimate way to police paying students? Were they out of their minds?

Claire threw back her covers and stomped toward the door. She could feel an angry flush flaring in her cheeks. "I thought you'd been told to stop harassing me!" she shouted through the door. "I'm not hiding my boyfriend in here, so just go away and leave me alone!"

Claire was about to turn away from the door when the loud knocking resumed. This time she turned around and yanked the door open, planning to pelt Julie with threats until she was reduced to tears, if necessary.

But when she opened the door, it wasn't Julie Sontay, her RA, at all.

It was Aaron Mendel.

Both of them stood there in silence for a moment.

"Who," Aaron said, stepping back slightly on one foot as if to regain his balance, "is the boyfriend you aren't hiding?"

"Aaron!" Claire gasped.

"Is it me?" Aaron asked hazily, bracing his arm on the doorjamb and leaning slightly forward. He was wearing a rumpled dark jacket and sunglasses and had a two days' growth of beard.

Claire barely recognized him. "Aaron, I . . ."

"God, I've missed you," he said suddenly, pulling off his sunglasses, gathering her around the waist, and kissing her hard on the lips.

Claire pulled back and looked into his hazel eyes. "God, Aaron, you're . . . wasted."

"I'm drunk and I'm tired," he slurred. "We had to cut our gig in Chicago short and come back on a bus. What a drag."

"Why did you cut it short?"

Aaron looked at her. "Because we weren't drawing huge crowds, that's why, Claire."

Claire felt him stumble toward her, and she instinctively held her hands up for him to stop. "Wait. I can't have any guys in here after eleven."

Aaron's handsome face dropped. "You're not going to invite me in?" he asked with a leer.

Claire hesitated.

"You aren't, are you?" Aaron repeated, the realization apparently rousing him out of his stupor. He had a strange, almost victorious look in his eyes. "Are you?"

"It's against the rules," Claire said weakly.

"Excuse me," Aaron said with mock dignity, pushing her aside and walking into her room.

Claire closed her eyes and leaned back against the doorjamb. There was a moment of silence as Aaron went in the room and took in the scene.

"Hello, Jake," Aaron said calmly, crossing his arms across his chest.

"It's not what you think," Claire said bitterly.

Aaron lifted his hands up in protest. "Oh. I'm so sorry. Please explain, *why* is Jake McRoyan sleeping half naked in your room right now?" His eyes darkened, and Claire could see him wobble slightly in the dim light.

"Stop it," Claire said quietly. She was beginning to worry that Aaron would do something. He was drunk enough.

Claire glanced over and saw that Jake had propped himself up in bed. He lifted his bare arm to shield himself from the light Aaron had just switched on. "Aaron?" Jake asked.

"Hello, handsome," Aaron said easily, but his eyes were narrowed with frightening intensity.

"He's staying here because he doesn't have a dorm room, Aaron," Claire cried out. "Nothing's going on between us!"

"Yeah," Aaron said slowly, standing over Jake with a menacing look. "Yeah, right." He turned to Claire, his face full of bitterness. "Naturally I believe that since you're both so trustworthy—"

"Watch it, Mendel," Jake said in a low voice. He got out of bed and glared at Aaron. "This is Claire's room."

"That, Jake—you idiot—is exactly my point. And I would like to know what you're doing here." Aaron drew his face near Jake's.

"Get out of here, Aaron," Claire warned. "We'll talk in the morning."

Aaron pulled his face closer to Jake's, then pushed him lightly in the chest with the tips of his fingers. "You think you're pretty tough, don't you, Jake?" He pushed Jake again.

Jake held up his hands. "Back off."

Claire saw Aaron's fist fly out before she could step between them. It hit Jake's mouth right at the corner, sending him back onto the bed. A trickle of blood made its way down Jake's chin.

A second later Jake was up again, and before Aaron could punch him again, Jake had twisted Aaron's right arm behind his back and was holding him in a firm lock. "Claire asked you to leave, remember? I think it's about time you were going." Jake shoved Aaron away in disgust.

Claire felt tears of frustration springing to her eyes. "Nice going, Aaron. I'm really impressed. I can't believe you!"

"Don't talk to me about what you can believe," Aaron spat. Suddenly his face softened. "I don't need this, Claire," Aaron said wearily. "I've been on the road for four weeks, I'm beat,

I'm ever so slightly drunk, and I want my girl-friend back."

"You don't trust me at all, do you?" Claire said simply. "What I'm saying about Jake needing a room means nothing to you. Did you notice that there are *two* beds in this room and that *both* of them have been slept in? Did you think we were moving from bed to bed?"

Aaron looked from one bed to the other. He said nothing.

Claire made a step back. "Get out of here."

Aaron waved her away and started to sit down. "Oh, right."

Claire's eyes grew hot. She couldn't believe this was the same handsome, in-control Harvard freshman she'd met only a year before. Aaron Mendel had been the only guy she'd ever met on Chatham Island who had enough of an edge to keep her interested. Things got very peculiar, though, when his mother married Burke Geiger. But that ended up bringing Claire and Aaron closer together. Then, strangely, as time went on, that turned into a deeper connection she'd begun to think of as love. It was amazing, Claire suddenly realized, how quickly a feeling like that could evaporate.

"I'm sorry, but you've got to leave," Claire whispered. "Now."

"You tell me to leave, and it's over."

Claire bit her lower lip to keep it from quivering. She took a breath. "Too late."

Aaron turned on his heel. "I hope you don't regret this. It's going to be pretty awful around the Thanksgiving table in a couple of months."

"Yeah. I guess so," Claire said quietly. "But probably no worse than usual."

Eighteen

Lara sits on a sandy beach with Mr. and Ms. Passmore, watching the sun set over the channel and the tree-fringed horizon beyond Weymouth. Her easel is propped on the warm sand, and as gentle waves lap at her toes she is painting the fiery colors of the sky, burning orange, red, and gold between purple streaks of cloud.

Though she is not looking at the Passmores, she can feel the warmth of their encouraging whispers beside her. She feels bathed in happiness, as if the air itself contained the feeling.

There is a subtle change in the atmosphere as she stands back to admire her work. On the canvas the sky rages crimson and scarlet. But as she looks up over the lip of her picture, she sees the sun blazing even hotter as it dips to the horizon. The colors burn her eyes with their brightness.

She continues to watch, transfixed, as the sun appears to ignite the trees it touches on its way down. A curling smoke appears in the sky, and she reaches for her paintbrush, overwhelmed by a sudden need to change the picture to match the quickly changing scene.

She hears the Passmores calling her as the gray of the smoke begins to overtake the bright sky, and a blood-red tide emerges from below it, spreading itself across the water to the sand, where she is standing.

"Hurry. Hurry. Hurry."

Lara begins to feel the heat on her face as she races to adjust her painting. She turns to look at the Passmores and sees to her horror that they have been overcome by the smoke. She turns to face the water again and realizes that the red tide is not water at all but a sheet of flame, racing quickly toward her and the Passmores.

Lara grabs her brushes and paints, then runs up the beach.

"Hurry. Hurry. Hurry!" she screams.

Her toes dig into the hot sand as she hears the sizzling sound of the flames reaching the beach, turning rose and white as they race even more quickly toward them.

A sudden cool sensation trickles down her leg, and Lara looks down, realizing that her paintbrushes are running with water. Though the smoke in her lungs has weakened her, she turns to beat back the sparks surrounding the Passmores with the wet brushes, raining drops of moisture into the sand.

She tries to lift them up, but they wave her on. "Hurry. Hurry. Hurry."

Smoke swirls around them, and Lara retreats in a panic toward the safety of the woods above the beach. And she realizes, all in a flash, as the flames blister her feet and the smoke engulfs the Passmores, that they are lost.

"Dad! Darla!" Lara screamed, sitting up in bed, raking the air with her hands.

She coughed and tears stung in her eyes, as if the dream had become real. She was flooded with relief when she realized it had only been the dream again, so vivid and terrifying, she could actually still smell the smoke from the flaming beach.

"Hurry," Lara whispered, drawing her hands up to her face. It had been the worst. The worst of her dreams so far.

Lara wiped her wet hands off on the top of the sheet, suddenly longing for Benjamin to be home. Benjamin had been right about so many things. He'd brought her together with her father. He'd seen her talent for painting. He'd believed that she had something to give when all anyone else could see was her dark side.

Benjamin saw a lot of things, Lara thought. And he'd been the one who'd been blind.

She let out a relieved sigh and set her head

back on her pillow, taking in a deep breath.

The smell. Lara sat up on her elbow. The smell from her dream was still there, though her nightmare was over. She coughed; then, her heart pounding, she turned over and looked out the dormer window, which was flickering with light.

For a moment Lara was paralyzed, not knowing whether she was in the midst of a dream, dreaming that she had awakened, or whether she really was conscious and watching something that was real.

She groped for Zoey's bedside light and flicked it on, praying for the smell of smoke and firelight in the window to disappear. But as light flooded the room she realized with horror that the black smoke seeping through the bottom of the closed bedroom door was as real as anything she'd ever seen in her life.

Lara leaped out of the bed and threw open the window. Below, against the pitch-black of the night, she could see crazy, dancing orange shadows leaping from the kitchen and out onto the back patio.

Lara opened her mouth to scream, but as in her dreams she found that no sound would come out.

"Zoey?" Lucas called out, startled.

He sat up suddenly in his bed, his sheets

twisted around his legs and his back sweating against the mattress. His room was pitch-black and silent except for the green numbers on his digital clock, which read 3:34 A.M.

Zoey? he thought. He could almost feel her stare on him, as if she were standing there next to him in the dark room.

He stood up and snatched his bathrobe. No way he was going to let Zoey drive him crazy in the middle of the night. Zoey was the person he loved. She wasn't a ghost. Not that he could deny she was crowding his thoughts at the moment.

He shook his head and opened the door to the tiny hallway, heading downstairs for his mother's leftover apple things in the fridge—a familiar ritual that reminded him of Zoey. Zoey loved the apple things.

Lucas was taking his second bite when he strolled into the dark living room, which looked out over the water, a view that was always interrupted by the comforting sight of the Passmores' Cape Cod house just down the path.

Staring at the Passmore house was something he did a lot. But as he stood casually in front of the sliding glass door to the deck, there was something so drastically different about the view, he almost choked. A bright flame of orange was flicking its way out of the Passmores' kitchen window toward the bedroom window above.

Zoey's bedroom.

"*Mom!*" Lucas screamed, hurling himself up the stairs and pushing open her door. "*Call the fire department! The Passmores' house is on fire!*"

He stood there long enough to see his mother's stunned face rise from the pillow and her arm reach for the telephone, nodding an acknowledgment. Then he turned and hurtled down the stairs and out the front door.

"Mr. Passmore!" he screamed into the night, sprinting over the worn grass, through the gap in the fence, and down the narrow strip of dirt pathway that he'd followed a thousand times to Zoey's house. "Ms. Passmore!"

After that moment everything happening that night seemed to Lucas a dream. Though he was sprinting faster than he imagined possible, he was acutely conscious of the wet grass grazing his feet, the brightness of the stars in the inky sky, and the briny smell of the sea that swelled in front of him. Everything, in fact, that he'd ever felt seemed to both explode and slow down in that moment. The fire. The danger. Zoey's home. His love for her and her family.

It seemed to take forever to reach the house.

"*Fire!*" he screamed, nearly tumbling over

the tiny gate in the Passmores' picket fence as he lurched to a stop, struggling to open it. *"Wake up!"*

He looked up, his eyes already stinging with smoke, as the flames licked higher up the side of the house and a cloud blacker than the night billowed against the stars, glowing orange along its edges.

"Jeff! Darla! Lara!" he screamed, running toward the front door.

But the door remained closed. And there was no answer.

Nineteen

"Jeff! Darla!" Lara screamed, the nerves in her body slackening for a split second so that her voice could finally explode out of its silence. She twisted away from the window and rushed for the door of her bedroom.

Confusion seemed to choke her as much as the smoke that was seeping like black fog through the bottom of her door. Fire. Thoughts of fire. Dreams of fire. Was she dreaming or awake? She didn't know.

It didn't matter.

She had a sudden, sharp memory of an inner-city fair her mother and a boyfriend had taken her to when she was a little girl. The fire department had built a tiny demonstration house and they let groups of people inside while they released a kind of fake, chemical smoke. Lara remembered crawling through the hallway as the firefighters told her to hold her head down below the blowing, artificial smoke.

Keep your head down low in a fire. That's where the air is.

Lara's eyes were already swollen with tears and smoke. Flashing somewhere in the back of her mind was the knowledge that she could crawl out Zoey's dormer window and drop to safety. Escape was in one direction, but the silence on the other side of her door made her turn.

Mr. and Ms. Passmore. They slept with their door open to the hallway.

"Jeff . . . Darla . . . *Dad!*" Lara screamed, taking one last deep breath before grasping the doorknob to her room and pulling it open.

The force of the heat and smoke pouring toward her from the hallway would have taken her breath away if she hadn't already been holding it firmly in her lungs. The only light came from behind her. Ahead, the dark of the night was blotted out even further by the coal black of the smoke.

Lara dropped and groped blindly for the edge of the runner that extended the length of the short hallway between Zoey's room and her parents'. She felt the rough rug fibers skin her knees and the pain of her empty lungs searing her chest.

That's where the air is.

Lara dropped her mouth to the floor as she

scrambled forward. Then she took a short, scared breath and the feeling of brief relief. There had been air, thick and choking, but air. She crawled quickly forward past the stairwell, where, as she looked below, a faint orange light sputtered briefly into white and red.

Fear. Her body was numb with it. Yet she was conscious of a familiar, stubborn anger propelling her forward as it had a thousand times before into places even worse than this one. There was one thing Lara was sure of. She'd never been afraid to live on the edge. And now, she realized, her weird kind of courage might turn out to have a purpose after all.

"Wake up!" she screamed, dropping her head low again for another meager lungful. As she did her head slammed into the doorjamb of Jeff and Darla's room.

In an awful second she realized that there would be no answer or sound from them unless she somehow did something fast. She flashed on the arrangement of furniture. The foot of the bed maybe ten feet from the door.

Her cheek hit the floor again, and she sucked in a breath, this one black and choking. On battered knees she gagged, then battled her way forward, lunging and grasping until she felt flesh. A leg. She grabbed a handful of pajama leg and pulled strongly with her arms.

There was a moan and a loud thump in the darkness as a body crashed to the floor. She gasped and swooned for lack of air. Vaguely, from the fullness of muscle, she knew that the leg was her father's. Her fingers grasped around two solid ankles and she crawled back, pulling what seemed like the weight of ten boulders across a never-ending stretch of carpet. Lara yanked the body around the corner, where it stuck.

"Help!" she screamed, not knowing whether her next breath would sustain her. All she could see now was a suffocating blackness and the faces of her drawings staring back at her.

Like the faces of angels.

Lucas could feel the heat of the fire on his shoulder the first time he smashed it into the front door.

"Jeff! Darla!" he screamed, feeling the pain racing into his arm. Choking smoke was shooting into the sky, and he heard the terrible sound of exploding glass on the opposite side of the house.

Bracing himself once more with his bare, cut feet, he grabbed the brass handle and threw the full weight of his body against the solid door. There was the sound of barely cracking wood, then a splintering crackle as his body hit the wood over and over again.

Finally he felt the resistance of the wood sag and heard the crash of the door splitting in two and smashing down in front of him. Blistering, choking smoke blasted into his face.

"Jeff! Darla! Lara!" he screamed, groping for the wooden stair railing he'd touched a million times before in light.

Ahead he could see the orange, blue, and purple flames roaring upward in the kitchen at the end of the hall, and he knew in a second that his opening the front door could easily fuel it directly toward him.

Barely able to breathe the choking, burning air, he fought his way up the carpeted stairs, now littered with red-hot sparks that seared the bottoms of his feet.

"Take him!" he heard a girl's scream just as he felt a hard lump of body under his groping hands, sagging upside down at the top of the stairway.

"Lara!" Lucas shouted, though the sheer effort of shouting nearly choked him into unconsciousness. He lunged forward and felt desperately for body parts until the two shoulders were in front of him and he was able to hook his arms under them.

Lucas pulled for his life, having no idea whether the fireball had already reached the bottom of the staircase or whether there was time to yank the person outside. He did it, anyway—blind and choking. The solid shoulders. Mr. Passmore's. Zoey's father. There was a crash in the back of the house and a fierce cracking just as he pulled Mr. Passmore over the splintered door and out into the flickering light outside.

Lucas felt Mr. Passmore begin to move just as he dropped him onto the grass, and Lucas saw the whirling lights of the fire truck screaming toward him, sirens wailing. He took a deep, gasping gulp of air and turned back toward the front door.

Flames could be seen clearly inside the living room, and in the light from the fire trucks he could see the roof smoldering and hissing as if it were ready to explode with heat.

Lucas rushed back through the front door ahead of the rubber-suited volunteer firefighters, who were calling him back and running toward him with still empty hoses.

"Get back, Cabral," one of the men shouted over the roar of the fire. "We're taking over."

Lucas recognized the voices, as he recognized every voice on this island. Pete Cennarusa, Buddy Evans, and Nick Dakin. He knew who they were. Overweight, fortyish volunteers who had neither the strength nor the stamina nor the will to go back in there where he was headed.

And Lucas was the only one who knew where to go.

Lara found herself moving in slow motion, not knowing which way was up and which was down. She was at the end of a long, dark tunnel, and she had just passed her father forward through it toward the light at the end.

Someone had been waiting for him there. She had felt him being pulled away from her.

"Darla," Lara whispered to herself, turning around on her hands and knees. Sparks flew up the stairs, burning her face. There was no air anymore, and her lungs were bursting. Yet she felt strangely detached from the pain, as if she were someone else looking in.

Faces kept haunting her, and now it was Ms. Passmore's face that appeared before her in the smoke. The face of someone Lara could reach out to. Arms that had held her when there had been no obligation to.

Lara groped blindly for the doorway, moving slower than pitch toward the bed. Below she heard the smashing of glass and shouts. There was the sound of surging water and the sudden change in atmosphere, as if she'd put her head over a pan of boiling water.

She lunged again for the bed through the

blinding storm of smoke, finding a soft waist. A shoulder. A wrist. She grabbed it and pulled forward, her bare feet slipping, then miraculously holding. She heard yelling near. Her name being called.

Lara held the wrist and dragged until she heard the drop of the body against the hard floor. As she had with her father, she pulled through the doorway, then yanked hard until the torso swung around to the staircase, headfirst.

She heard something far away. Her name, maybe. Whirling lights. A cracking sound. Then the weight of Darla's body lifting away from her like the wind.

Lara was using her arms now to pull forward, perhaps to follow the body down the stairs; she wasn't sure. The heat had made her sleepy, and the dreams had begun again, just like the others. Dreams of fire. Dreams of the heat and danger and people she loved just ahead of her, calling her forward.

She would reach them soon. A good thing, Lara thought in her dream, because now she knew that she loved them.

And she was ready to tell them so.

Because the flames had jumped from the front hallway over the stair railing and were racing upstairs, Lucas was sure that Ms.

Passmore and Lara were lost.

The fire had held steadily in the kitchen and living room for too long, and now the front entry appeared to be caving in under the force of the smoke and flame. He felt the grip of a hand on his arm, pulling him back.

"Move out, Cabral!" someone shouted. "This place is going up."

Lucas shook off the hand and muscled away into the darkness, crawling into the flame, his feet still bare and his lungs charred with smoke. The only thing he really saw or cared about was the image of Zoey's face in front of him. The face she would have if she was told her mother was dead. It was impossible for him to consider. It couldn't happen to Zoey. It couldn't happen to the Passmores.

He held his arms in front of his face against the flames, then, unbelievably, found a small tunnel of an opening along the wall of the staircase. Just enough to squeeze forward and grab anything—please, God, anyone—who might be trying to get down.

"Darla! Lara!" he shouted.

Then, just as he couldn't take another step, Ms. Passmore's face appeared out of the smoke on the stairway in front of him. It had banged down hard and was now hanging upside down, slack jawed, charred, and unconscious. A reddening bruise ran along one cheek. He grabbed her under the armpits and pulled with all his strength, all the time aware of the gray outline of the slender girl he had seen just behind Ms. Passmore on the staircase.

There was the realization that someone was helping him from below. There were shouts. Ms. Passmore's weight was lifted away.

He turned to go back for the shadow above on the staircase, but as he did there was the sound of a huge explosion, as if a match had been touched to gunpowder and the world began to cave in around him.

"Darla's alive!" he heard someone shout in the distance.

An arm slipped around his body, pulling him back just as the staircase collapsed and burst into a ball of flame, throwing him backward out the door. His back hit the grass, and the cool night air suddenly flooded his lungs.

But up ahead he could see that the fire—orange, crimson, and white—had taken over, consuming everything that had been left behind, lighting the sky up like a beacon.

The twenty-sixth title in the fabulous
MAKING OUT series:

Zoey's broken heart. What can anyone say to
make it feel better? Because the disaster that
destroyed Zoey's home and injured her parents,
has left Zoey devastated. And she's still so far
from Lucas . . .

Zoey's broken heart

Falling for Claire

MAKING WAVES,
the hot new series by the author of
MAKING OUT

Florida is everything Summer Smith had dreamed of.
The sun is scorching, the water is brilliant blue, and
the guys are tanned and gorgeous. Will this be her
summer of love?